THE DOCTO...

THE DOCTOR

THE DOCTOR

BY
ISABEL CAMERON

" The pure in heart shall see God."

Thirty-eighth Impression

LUTTERWORTH PRESS
LONDON

PRINTED IN GREAT BRITAIN BY THE WHITEFRIARS PRESS LTD.
LONDON AND TONBRIDGE

FOREWORD

In sending forth this new and enlarged edition of *The Doctor*, the publisher asked me to write a Foreword. " But what shall I say ? " I asked in dismay. " Oh, anything," he replied easily. " People never read Forewords, they're just put in for the look of the thing." Thus reassured, I take up my pen to thank all those who have given the little book such a warm welcome. The writing of it has been a sheer labour of love, and if I have managed to capture and to convey to the reader some stray gleams of the winsome personality of the original, then I am content.

His friendship enriched my life, and gladdened my heart, and has left an abiding memory at once gracious, tender, and gladsome. One cannot recall the Doctor without a smile creeping into one's eyes. Coming to our house as he did at a time when the shadow of illness lay on it, his is a tender and an especially warm place in our hearts. " What ! " he would say in pretended amazement, when I would tell him of the invalid's improvement. " *He's not dead yet !* He's a fraud, a malingerer ! I'll report him to the Presbytery ! " But at evening prayers, how he would pour forth thanks to the great Father God for restoring health and courage, and how near we felt the Unseen at such moments ! So, with laughter and with tears (and are they not twin sisters ?) our friendship grew closer and closer.

His views of God were like himself, great and spacious. " Money," he cried one day, " it's just God's gift to His children who can't understand anything better. He gives them money to play with, just as we give little children ha'pennies to please them. But to His own dear children, He gives His great gifts, wisdom and understanding so that they see wondrous things out of His law. These are the things that matter because they abide." A comforting thought in these days of materialism.

So the Doctor rests from his labours but his works do follow him. In the Old Book he loved so well it is written " The memory of the just is blessed."

ISABEL CAMERON

THE DOCTOR'S BIRTHDAY

IT was a windy, sunny March morning. In the quiet street where the old minister, Dr. Lindsay, lived, two message boys were enjoying a game of football, an ancient syrup tin serving as a ball. The tin, with the hollow sound peculiar to empty cans, landed just at the Doctor's feet as he closed the gate behind him. He was feeling particularly gay this morning. It was his birthday, and the post had brought him all sorts of remembrances from loving friends. Perhaps the one which pleased him most was from his granddaughter, who was training as a teacher of cookery in Edinburgh. She sent him a box of cakes of her own baking, and each a perfect triumph of culinary art. "Far too pretty to eat," the old Doctor decided. "Tut, tut, why is the bairn worrying about me having to pay her fees ? Silly lassie ! "

His heart was warm with the thought of these things as he stepped out and found the tin at his feet. With a quick look up and down the street to satisfy himself that no one was watching him, and settling his soft hat more firmly on his white head, he gave a hop, step, and leap, and sent the tin hurtling merrily back to the astonished errand boys. These admirable youths were picking up their various baskets, with a " life-is-real-life-is-earnest " expression, but they could not repress their admiration for the Doctor's sportsman-like shot. With a yell of delight the butcher's hireling (known as " that limb o' Tulloch's ") sent the tin flying back, and the Doctor, now fairly into his stride, returned it with such energy it went headlong into the grocer boy's basket, where it instantly converted a dozen fresh eggs into custard or omelette—just as you chose to look at it. The " limb o' Tulloch's " had also suffered in the fray, and the leg of mutton which had been entrusted to his tender mercies rolled helplessly in the dust. Without wasting time, he seized it and, adjourning to the nearest pump, he gave it a vigorous sousing, and then dried it with the blue-striped apron with which butcher-boys are generally girded. He thoughtfully offered the use of the garment to the grocer's loon " to wipe things wi'."

If you think the Doctor was dismayed by this accident you don't know him in the least. His was an eternal and a joyous youth, which rose triumphant over trifles. " Where were you going, my boy ? " he inquired, and his brown eyes were twinkling like a mischievous child's.

" To the Manse, sir."

The Doctor chuckled. " That's all right ! Tell the housekeeper that it was my fault, and tell her, too, that she's to give you a cake each out of the box that came this morning." By what magical sleight-of-hand both boys found themselves in possession of pennies it is not for me to say, and long before the loons had thought of suitable words of thanks he was half-way down the street.

Life became once more for these harassed and hard-working young men a grim reality ; yet were their hearts warm and grateful because of " him who passed."

The years in their flight had brought much added sweetness and wisdom to the old Doctor, but his heart was always the heart of a child. That was the reason why all children smiled when he came near them. There were two little children playing with a wheelbarrow, and as the Doctor passed he laid his hand upon the head of the smaller one. Though he spoke no word, the bairn seemed to divine that he blessed him, and so did his brother, for he came running after the old saint and said timidly, " Dae't to me, too ! "

" Dae what ? "

" What ye did to ma wee brither," the child pleaded. " Lay your hand on my heid."

Somehow the pathetic words uttered in the old time by an elder brother, as he pleaded with his father for a blessing, flashed into the Doctor's remembrance, " Bless me, even me also, O my father." His generous heart was quick to answer the appeal, and he laid his kindly hand upon the child's rough head, and blessed him.

His first call was at the house of Mary Mackenzie, a woman stricken down with a sore and grievous illness. For weeks she had been slowly dying, but to the woman, a Highlander, brought up in orthodox Ross-shire, the supremely important question was, was she one of the elect? This, more than the pain of her trouble, more than the thought of death even, oppressed her.

" How are you to-day ? " the old Doctor asked as he sat down by her bedside. " No pain ? And you rested well and slept for an hour or two ? That is good news. The Father is dealing gently with His child."

The sick woman sighed, and the look in her eyes told more than her tongue. " It's a long, dark road I will have to be going," she whispered. For a minute the Doctor did not speak. Then taking her hand in his he said, " I mind when I was a little laddie we lived a good way out of the town, and one night I had been sent a message and it was dark before I got home. The road lay through a dark wood, and, of course, I was sure there was a bogie behind every tree waiting to gobble me up ; and when I heard a footstep, then I was quite sure I was doomed ; but before I could yell, I heard a voice saying, ' Is that you, Willie ? ' It was my father. He was looking for me when I was never thinking about him, and the road was short and as light as day because he was with me. It was only my earthly father—and he had been anxious about his boy. Don't you think, Mary, that the heavenly Father, who puts the love into our hearts, is willing to come with us on our dark roads ? ' I will not leave you comfortless,' He said, ' I will come to you.' ' When thou passest through the waters I will be with thee.' "

In text after text he poured forth his soul, and the sick woman at last caught some of the ecstasy of his spirit and smiled, albeit tremulously. The tears were running down her cheeks, but it was the thaw after the long black frost.

" Mary," he said, " is it not well with you ? He's calling you ! He's saying, ' *Mary, is this you at last ? I have been looking for you for years.*' "

There are those yet who remember the old Doctor's prayers—the near and dear intimate talk of a child speaking to a beloved parent—for the Fatherhood of God was ever to him the supreme thing.

Mary was sobbing softly when he finished and when Kate Murray, who lived in the other end of the house and looked after Mary, stole to the door, she was amazed to hear the old Doctor singing in his voice which was still sweet,

> " When Zion's bondage God turned back,
>   As men that dreamed were we."

It seemed to Kate, as she stole softly away, that she heard the clink as of coins changing hands, and she certainly heard Mary protesting, " But there is no occasion, sir. I have the old-age pension, and it's more than I ever made with spinning or knitting."

When the Doctor emerged from Mary's, he took his way round the corner and past the smithy, which was shut up. John, the smith, when he caught sight of Dr. Lindsay, instantly became so engrossed in his work (which happened to be the mending of a broken slate on the roof) that he could not even raise his eyes. His careless unconsciousness of the minister's presence was a trifle too elaborate. With quite unnecessary violence he began to hammer in a nail, and did it with such vigour that he broke the slate. It fell with a loud clatter, and John's little boy, a child of four, who had been playing about the foot of the ladder, screamed. Like a flash of lightning the Doctor darted in, and by what was nothing short of a miracle, he swept the child into a place of safety. The child's mother with a white, scared face came running out. " It's all right," the Doctor said, carrying the child into the house, "Johnnie is all right ; aren't you, boy ? "

By this time the father had descended and joined them. "Is—is—the bairn—a' richt?" he faltered.

"All right," Dr. Lindsay replied cheerfully, "neither cracked nor broken. Tell your Daddy, Johnnie, that you are all right."

John, the smith, suddenly sat down, and wiped his brow. "I . . . nearly . . . killed . . . ma . . . bairn . . ." he faltered, "I meant that slate for—for . . ."

"Ay, ay," said the Doctor comfortably, "you don't snuff, do you? Try a pinch," offering a snuff mull which on many an occasion tided over an awkward pause in a conversation.

But John, having started to confess, was determined to make a clean breast of things. "I nearly killed ma wife on Setterday," he said; "I came home drunk— you needna hide your face, Maggie, ye ken it's true, and that it was ma hand that . . ."

"Hush, hush," she cried piteously, "dinna let the bairn hear you!"

"And noo I nearly killed ma bairn," he went on stubbornly.

"I always have hopes of a man when I hear him confessing his sins," the Doctor said cheerfully. "It's the man who confesses other men's sins that I cannot thole."

He did not spare John in the talk that followed, but he sent his wife and child out of the room first. Then he dealt faithfully with the man but, like the skilful surgeon he was, he did not inflict one unnecessary incision, and very tenderly he bound up the wound afterwards.

"If you can spare the time," he was saying as he came out of the room, "you might take a look at the roof of my kitchen. There's a bit of it leaky, and you know the old word says, ' *Thekk your roof in the calm.*' Johnnie, boy, could you run up to the Manse and tell my housekeeper that I sent you for some of the nice cakes I got this morning?"

And Johnnie, with a beaming face, scampered off.

Beyond the smithy, and just before the Doctor turned up the road to Sweetmeadows, he met Meg the henwife swinging along with a basket of eggs over her arm.

" Well, Margaret, how are you ? " he said, stopping and holding out his hand, ' I'm glad to see that you are well, though I haven't seen you in church for some time."

Meg's manner was haughty. " I haff my reasons," she said with her nose in the air. She came from distant Stornoway, and spoke the English language in a fascinating way, agreeable to all if intelligent only to herself. " I haff my reasons," she repeated, but the frost in her manner was visibly melting, for who could withstand the Doctor when he looked at you with his friendly brown eyes ?

" I am glad you have your reasons," he said solemnly (though his eyes laughed). " From what I know of you, I am sure they are good ones, too. May I hear them ? "

" It is about my seat in the church," Meg burst forth. " They haff moved me from the transvaal where I wass sitting and they have put me into the seat of the merchant, and I am ferry angry, because I wass sitting yonder since the resurrection."

" And so you are not coming to church," the Doctor said musingly.

Meg grew uncomfortable. " It is not of the same quality," she went on ; but what she meant, one can only dimly conjecture.

" Ay," the Doctor said in a tentative fashion, " I see." Then he cleared his throat. " Did I ever tell you why the kirk-session of Kincorn all resigned ? " he asked. " Well, the reason was almost as good as yours—the session clerk's wife gave a clocking hen to the ruling elder's wife to hatch out chickens, and the hen would not sit and broke the eggs, so the wife stayed from the church and made her man stay too ; and then the other wife heard of this, and she stayed from church and so did

her husband, and the bairns stopped coming to the
Sunday School, and the end of the matter—— "

"But that was ferry wrong," Meg interrupted.
"Many's the hen I haff that will not sit s'pose I wass to
kill her. If that wife had had sense—— "

The Doctor laughed. "Ay, if she had had sense,"
he echoed, "like you Margaret, and came to the
church and took care of her soul and never heeded her
temper."

Meg had the grace to laugh, "You must excuse me,
sir, for making so free, but I'm sinking I'll be coming
back to the church."

"That's right! I'll speak to the seat-letting folk to
give you back your old seat."

"Not at all, not at all," cried Meg. "It wass myself
that was complaining, I could not hear you sitting in
yon transvaal; but I wass not wishing to sit wiss the
merchant, for he once cheated me out of half a dozen
eggs."

"And how much was that?" Dr. Lindsay said,
putting his hand into his pocket. Meg uttered a shrill
expostulation, and turned hurriedly away. "Well,
call at the Manse and ask my housekeeper to give you
a cup of tea, and one of my grand cakes, when you are
done of selling your eggs," the Doctor called after her
as they took their separate ways.

Into the farmhouse of Sweetmeadows the old Doctor
came like sunshine in a November fog. The farmer had
been chained to his bed with a broken leg for six weeks.
In a "farm toon" the work is always "thrang" in the
spring, and James Falconer chafed at being thus imprisoned, "like a tethered hen," as he expressed it.

He was full of questions as to what Burnbraes on his
right hand, and Bruntland on the left, and Burnside
over the way were doing; how the ploughing was
getting on; how the lambs were looking, and what
appearance had the young grass. And because the
Doctor had spent his earliest days on a farm, he was able
to answer all the questions satisfactorily.

"If I could only get my legs below me," Falconer sighed.

"How many years had you your legs below you?" the minister asked with a kindly twinkle in his eye, "and did you always thank the Lord for it? We take His gifts as a matter of course; but when He withholds one, we cry out in dismay. Oh, I know! I do it myself! The other day I was out for a turn, and because it was such a sunny morning I took my newspaper and sat down by the riverside. Well, suddenly it began to rain, and I had neither coat nor umbrella, so what did I do but make a hole in the middle of my paper and stick my head through it. It came round my shoulders like a lampshade, but it kept me dry! Well, I was stepping home when I met a lad driving a young horse, and at the sight of my lampshade the beast bolted. (I think it was one of the Bruntland horses). The lad and myself gave chase, and at last we caught him. 'I'm afraid I frightened your horse?' I said. 'Frichtened the horse,' says the lad. 'You wad frichten the very deil, going aboot like that.' 'Well, my boy,' says I, 'I have been trying to frighten the devil for fifty years, and he's not scared of me yet.' Neither he is, for when I went home and felt rheumatism in my back, the devil whispered to me that it was wonderful how God afflicted me, and I nearly believed him till I minded it was not God at all, but my own foolhardihood for sitting on the damp grass."

There was a subtle undermeaning in this little story, which James Falconer, a worthy man but perhaps a little too worldly, was not slow to see. "When I get my legs again," he said cheerfully, "we must see about getting some alterations done to the church. It's a disgrace to think how long it is since there was a lick of paint put on it." And the Doctor, well pleased with the result of his little sermon, took his departure.

Falconer's ploughman was standing smoking in the barn door as he passed, and he responded gruffly to the Doctor's genial greeting. He was one of that fast-

growing band who do not approve of ministers and
scarcely ever enter a church. His manner was antago-
nistic and repellant as the minister paused to ask after
his health.

"It's a long time since I have seen you in church,"
Dr. Lindsay said—" not since I christened your last
baby."

The man grunted and did not trouble to remove his
pipe.

"I don't approve of churches," he said sourly.

"Look at the way you ministers quarrelled over the
Union. Do you mean to tell me that is right? I'm a
common working grieve, but mind, I'm telling you, I
took a scunner at the kirks then, and now they're speaking
aboot anither union. Well, let them go at it! Jock
Bruce and myself were near han' at blows one
day here aboot this union." He paused and looked
righteously indignant.

"How many bairns have you?" the Doctor asked
with seeming irrelevance.

"Six, sir."

"All christened?"

"They are that," he replied proudly.

"You remember when you held up your children in
baptism you promised to bring them up in the nurture
and admonition of the Lord; are you doing it?"

"I'm doing it as well as most; look at Burnbraes'
ploughman——"

"We'll just look at you, William," the Doctor said
quietly. "There was that nice laddie of yours who
went to Vancouver (I have a letter of his in my pocket,
I'll give you to read. Yes, poor boy, he sent back the
passage money I lent him). Well, when he was going
away, I said, 'Mind, Willie, and say the prayers you
learnt at your mother's knee.' What think you did he
say? 'I never learnt any prayers at my mother's
knee; the only prayer ever I learnt was the one yourself
taught me in the Sunday School.'"

William's pipe was in his pocket long ago and his face

was red as he listened. " Now, I'm an old man and you're a young one—well, you are young beside me— to-day is my seventy-eighth birthday—so you can take a word of advice from me. Never mind finding fault with the rest of the world, just try to make your own corner of it as happy as you can. I'll be looking for yourself and your wife and the bairns in the church next Sunday. That's the sort of Church Union I'm asking the Lord to let me see before I go hence. Here's the letter, and you can give it back to me the next time you come to see me."

The heart had died out of the day when the old man turned his face homeward. He had grown tired and faint, and with the shades of night a sense of his own loneliness oppressed him. His wife had died years ago, and his children were all in homes of their own. Before the emptiness and desolation of his own fireside, his bright, brave spirit quailed. " Father, take me home soon," he whispered like a tired child, as he sat down wearily in his chair. He shut his eyes, and for a moment a tide of longing broke over him, leaving him drenched and miserable.

His housekeeper tapped at the door. " Dan Angus is in the kitchen, sir, wanting to see you ; but maybe you'll have your supper first."

In a minute the tiredness fell from him like a mantle. Dan had been in the " far country," and the mere fact that he had voluntarily sought the minister, told that Dan's face was turned once more to the Father's house.

" You did well to keep him, Janet. Bring him and the supper too ! " he cried.

He greeted his visitor with kindness, but without any appearance of being astonished.

The Father had answered another of his prayers, that was all.

" Janet," he cried, " bring me the box of cakes I got this morning."

Janet, a long-suffering and silent woman, allowed herself one remark. " I can bring you the box——"

she said. The old Doctor opened it and peeped among its paper linings. There was one small and rather limp-looking cake left. He took it out and handed it to his visitor.

" You take it," he said, " I have meat to eat that ye know not of."

THE DOCTOR "VISITS"

I

THE Doctor knocked gently at the door.

"How is your father to-day, Miss Forsyth?" he asked.

"He's real dottled kind, Doctor; come awa in an' see him."

She led the way into the sick-room. "D'ye ken wha this is, faither?" she asked the little old man in the bed. "This is Dr. Lindsay come to see you."

The old man's face beamed with pleasure. "Oh, weel div I ken him! A fine man—the finest man ye could fa' in wi'."

The daughter, with a scandalised face, turned to the Doctor apologetically. "Did I no' tell ye?" she sighed. "Ye can see for yersell how dottled he's grown! But ye needna wunner either—he's near a hunner years auld!"

The Doctor's eyes were dancing, but the rest of his face was quite solemn as he said, "I just hope when I'm as old I'll be as charitable in my judgments."

"Hoo's yersell?" the old man asked in his high piping voice. "What's doing in the toon?"

In his younger days Donald Forsyth had been a slater, and it was pathetic to hear how persistently the old man's thoughts turned back to his working days. Now the Doctor was able to tell him all about a new school which was being built near, and how the carpenters that very morning had been fixing the joists for the roof.

"The sclaters will be on gin the end o' the week," the old man said, and there was a wistful look in his face. "Man, I sometimes wad gie onything jist for the feel o' the hammer an' the nails again—an' the smell o' the new wood an' the fresh lime, an' me astride

a roof ! I had a queer dream last nicht," he went on.
" I dreamt that I was young again, an' able for ma
wark, an' that I was sclating a hoose—a real bonnie
hoose, an' the maister came up to see it, an' says he,
' Are you near dune, Donald ? ' ' Aye,' I said. ' Aye,
sir, twa mair sclates 'll feenish ' ; and he says, ' That's
richt—I'm expectin' the tenant for the hoose vera
sune '—an', an'—steek the door, Doctor ; I dinna want
Janet to hear—the tenant's name was written ower the
door, an' wha's think ye was it ? "

He paused to search the Doctor's face for sympathy
and understanding.

" Ye're richt ! " he cried triumphantly (the Doctor
had not uttered a word, but his eyes were eloquent),
" Ye're quite richt, it was jist ma verra ain ! "   A great
smile lit up his face as he leaned back exhausted on his
pillow.

" That was a great dream, Donald," the Doctor said
softly, and then taking his little well-worn Bible out of
his pocket, he read : " *For we know that if the earthly
house of our tabernacle be dissolved, we have a building from
God, a house not made with hands, eternal in the heavens* " ;
and to the old man, whose earthly tabernacle was so
soon to be dissolved, the words brought great comfort
and cheer. The Master Builder seemed very near as
the Doctor gave thanks for the home of many mansions,
and the glad, strong life of the city, where the inhabi-
tants shall not say, " I am sick," and the oldest angels
are the youngest.

The old man seemed to doze as the Doctor stole
quietly away, with a whispered word of sympathy to
the daughter so soon to be left alone.

II

The sunny street was full of children hurrying home
for dinner. How the Doctor remembered their names
was a mystery—but remember them he did—and what
was even more surprising, he remembered the sex of

the little babies, who, in charge of mother or nurse, were taking the air. No mother ever forgives you if you call her baby " it " ; it is almost as unpardonable as calling her splendid boy " she ! "

One particularly delicious little dumpling, in all the pomp and circumstance of a white starched frock, was coming towards him in charge of her nurse. She stared solemnly at her old friend, and then announced, " *Noo soos*," pointing to her toes.

The Doctor expressed liveliest admiration.

" I've a clean hankie myself," he remarked with modest pride. He drew out the large, white, silk square with which we always associated him, for he was one of the daintiest of men. Strange to say, his handkerchief came forth accompanied by a square of butterscotch ! " Where could this have come from, I wonder ? " the Doctor murmured to himself. " It's most remarkable ! I wonder are there any more squares ? "

There were ! One for nurse and one for Molly—and with many wavings of Molly's fat little hands and kisses blown adown the wind, the little company parted. A lonely old maid who lived on the othe side of the street had been watching the little incident from behind her curtain. She sighed as they passed out of sight. Somehow, the street seemed forlorn and desolate now that they had gone.

III

The old pensioner who lived next door was tying up a rose tree, and the Doctor gave him a cheery greeting. " How are the roses, Peter ? "

" Fine, sir," Peter answered.

" And how's Mactavish ? " Mactavish was Peter's terrier, and loved by him as only an old bachelor can love a dog.

At this question Peter's face clouded. " That spiteful auld maid," he began.

"Meaning your next door neighbour, Miss Jane Brodie?" the Doctor interposed blandly.

"It's her," Peter said with much emphasis and no grammar. "She threw a brush at the poor sowl o' a dowg an' got him fair in the back! I'll have the law on her!"

"Mactavish was meantime chasing her cat?" the Doctor asked carelessly. Peter evidently did not hear. "It's the first time I ever heard of a woman managing to hit what she aimed at," the Doctor chuckled.

"She couldna weel miss him," the old soldier said bitterly. "She had him between her an' the water-tank."

"On the top of which her cat had taken refuge," the Doctor said shrewdly. "Aye, aye, Peter, we must live and let live. I always think of the way Miss Jane nursed her parents when they were dying. How good and dutiful she was. Her heart is gold, Peter. Yes, I believe she is a real child of God—a daughter of the King all glorious within."

"Then," said Peter, determined to have his revenge, "*them that auchts her sud flipe her!*"

It was too much for the Doctor! His shouts of laughter brought both Miss Jane and the injured Mactavish out to investigate. "Dinna lat on," Peter pleaded; but the Doctor was helplessly wiping his eyes, incapable of speech; Mactavish, who was quite the gentleman if you kept him away from cats, joined politely in the laughter, so what else could the others do? No quarrel can raise its ugly head amidst innocent gaiety. When the Doctor parted with the neighbours, Peter was cutting a bunch of roses for Miss Jane, while that lady was patting Mactavish on the head and calling him "Good doggie!"

IV

The Doctor was humming a little tune to himself as he faced the country road, for he was doing his

" country rounds " this afternoon. It was a lovely sunny afternoon in June, and the world was looking very beautiful. The Doctor's face reflected the fairness of the day, and looked like a house whose open doors and windows are full of happy children and lovely flowers. Suddenly his expression changed ; it became dull and blank, as if one had put up dark shutters and closed the front door.

Coming towards him was Burgess of Burnbraes, driving into town. There are certain people who cannot be more fittingly described than by saying they are " nesty buddies," and to this unpleasant class belonged the mean-faced little man now approaching— a canine smile on his thin-lipped mouth, and the trustless expression of a ferret glinting out of his eyes.

With a great appearance of pleasure he drew rein. " I'm extra glad to see you, Doctor," he said with insincere gush. " I was determined to see you the day if I had to go to the Manse ! "

He gave a cackling unpleasant laugh, but there was no answering smile on the Doctor's face. Burnbraes shuffled uneasily in his seat, and in his heart he resented the Doctor's attitude and determined to have his revenge.

" If you have the time you might go and see poor David Anderson at the Haughs. He has been six weeks on his bed and neither minister nor elder has darkened his door."

" Aye," the Doctor's tones were non-committal, " the doctor is attending him, I suppose ? "

" Twice a day for a week or two," replied Burnbraes with much satisfaction.

" They sent a message for him ? "

" Ou, aye, the loon was once or twice for him through the night."

" Did they send a message to the minister ? "

Burnbraes had not seen what was coming and he was somewhat taken aback.

" I couldna—say—" he stammered.

" You know well enough they did not," the Doctor said sternly. " When David Anderson has a child to get baptised, he comes to church one Sunday before and whiles, one Sunday after, and that's all we see of him. When he's sick he sends for the doctor, but thinks the minister will miss him out of the church and will know by instinct that he is ill, and he will make himself believe that he's an ill-used man. Oh, I've heard David Anderson on the subject before."

" Aye," said Burnbraes, " I was sorry to hear the things he was saying about you."

" Why did you not come and tell me then ? "

" Oh, I was busy putting down the neeps, and couldna spare the time. I would excuse you, Doctor, if I was Davy, and say nothing about it ; but I was annoyed at the folks saying if it had been Gordon of the Burnside you would have been out lang syne seeing him, 'cause he's a big farmer and poor Davy is a small one, an'——"

With an uplift of the hand the Doctor silenced him. " I should certainly have missed Mr. Gordon," he said stiffly. " He's in church regularly. That I know. Whether he's a poor man or a rich one I have not the slightest idea. As a matter of fact, I am on my way to see David Anderson now. Fine weather, isn't it ? "

" Too dry—far too dry—if we dinna get rain the neeps will be spiled," replied the " nesty buddy," who was never known to be pleased with the weather.

With a coldly polite bow the Doctor went on his way, his spirit jarred and rasped by this encounter. " Such men are in every congregation," he used to say. " God allows them there for the minister's sanctification." The wind had shifted to the east, and the sun had gone behind a cloud.

V

The Doctor was walking along soberly enough now— when at the cross-roads he met a company of tinkers— brown-faced men and women and children. and, because he never could resist speaking to a baby, he must needs stop and ask the names and ages of the little folks. " This little one now ? " he asked pointing to a bundle carried by a young mother. " How old is your baby, my dear ? "

" She's only three weeks auld." Proudly she unrolled the bundle, disclosing a small red face and a pair of bright eyes. She listened with outward carelessness (but inward pride) to the Doctor's praise of her first-born, and " What is her name ? " he asked.

" She's no chrissened yet, sir," she said, and then, because for her child a mother can be greatly daring, she faltered, " Would you, sir, chrissen her ? "

The Doctor stood for a moment in thought. " Is your husband here ? " he asked.

" Yes, sir. Wull, stand forrit ! " A tall, sheepish young man came forward, touching his forelock as he came.

" And here's ma lines," said the young mother, now as brave as a lion (so to speak), and produced from some mysterious keeping place her marriage lines and the child's birth certificate.

After the Doctor had examined them he said, " Well, friends, we'll just have a word of prayer."

Overhead a choir of larks sang their rapturous song of praise. Against the soft blue of the sky the dark sombre green of the fir trees and the tender green of the birches made a fitting background for this strange little company. The brown burn, slipping softly by, seemed to croon a happy contented lilt, carrying the news to the far distant sea that once again the Master was saying, " Suffer little children to come unto Me, and forbid them not." As the Doctor stood with bare white head and reverend face, the tinker folk felt the spell of the Unseen touching their hearts. This Friend, present but unseen, to Whom the old minister spoke with such love and confidence, might they not catch a glimpse of Him too ? If they could have put their thoughts into speech they would have used the words of the old time when one said, "Did not our heart burn within us while He talked with us by the way?"

An old woman, evidently the baby's grandmother, had dipped a jug into the brown burn, and with water warmed by the sun and soft from some distant ben, Mary Stewart got her name. The baby wailed a little at the name—perhaps she knew what a tragic one it is in Scotland; perhaps it was because her father did not hold her comfortably.

The Doctor's pockets were always standing open for the benefit of those who might choose to put their hands into them, and now from one of them he took a white penny and put it into the baby's tiny hand. There was a shower of brown pennies for the other children, and then, followed by the blessings and thanks of the whole tribe, he took the road again. And because of him who passed, and tarried with them for a little while, the hearts of these poor aliens and outcasts were softened and humanised as only hearts can be touched by the winsomeness and the wonder of Divine love.

VI

At the farther end of the wood the Doctor came on Willie Gills herding a dejected-looking cow.

"How are you, Willie?" the Doctor shouted—for William was deaf beyond all telling. Often, too, he misunderstood what was said, which made conversation with him a thing of great surprises.

"Very sick, sir," he replied, evidently thinking the Doctor had asked about the cow. "So's the wife, and 'deed I'm no' awful weel masell."

"Tut, tut!" said the Doctor sympathetically.

"It's this evil new fashions, sir, that did it," Willie went on in the peculiar toneless voice of the very deaf. "If folk wad be wearing iron clamps on their heels, ma coo was well the day."

The Doctor looked bewildered. "Aye?" he shouted.

"Just that," Willie said. "Iron clamps is na good

enuff noo. Folk maun hae this *ginger rubbon* heels on their boots, an' that's what no coo can digest." He spat viciously and nodded his head. "What no coo can digest," he repeated.

"Did your cow eat a rubber heel?" the Doctor shouted. "Was that what made her sick?"

"Wha?" Willie asked. "Is't the wife you're asking aboot? She's no weel wi' eating too muckle curds."

"But what made the cow sick?"

"Sick? It's no sick so muckle as severe pain in the pit o' ——"

"Yes, yes," the Doctor said hastily. "The cow I'm asking about."

"Spent a hale day ower one boot," Willie said gloomily, "an' then near choked on the ginger rubbon heel." With a sympathetic handshake the Doctor left him, not at all clear in his mind as to which of William's household had been emulating the ostrich.

VII

There was a long dreary stretch of road to walk ere reaching the little farm of the Haughs, where David Anderson lay ill. The weary-faced woman who came in answer to his knock was David's wife, a gentle, diffident little creature whose spirit had long ago been broken by her domineering, hectoring husband.

"When had you a night in your bed?" the Doctor asked gently, clasping her hand in his own warm, friendly grip. At the kind words her eyes filled with sudden tears.

"I have aye to watch at nights," she said, with a catch in her throat; "but Davy's mendin' noo, an' sleepin' too."

"Did you ever hear, Mrs. Anderson, that ' His angels watch over him who sleeps, but with the watcher a watch He keeps '? Not lonely the night when He is keeping watch too."

" Aye, sir," she said, feeling her chafed soul already soothed, for David Anderson was an " ill " man to nurse.

The strangely sensitive spirit of the Doctor felt the hostile atmosphere when he entered the sick-room.

" So you've come at last," was the first salutation growled out by the beetle-browed man lying in bed. " Six weeks—aye, near seven—an' neither minister nor elder darkened my door."

The Doctor let him give vent to all the bitter thoughts which he had been cherishing and then when he was quite done he said pleasantly, " Well, David, you have been very frank with me, and I'll be equally frank with you. When were you in church last ? Just one Sunday after I baptised your last child—and the child is three years old. Do you mean to tell me that you had duties every Sunday since then, which kept you at home ? Still, when a man begins to confess the minister's faults, I have hopes of him. Perhaps—with the help of God—he may presently be confessing his own."

Very faithfully and very tenderly did he speak to the sick man, but he wounded only to bind up again. There was a shamed flush on the man's face which was all for his soul's good. His wife had crept in, and was sitting at the foot of the bed.

" When you're better, Davy," the Doctor said, " you and the good wife must go for a holiday. She's needing it as much as you. Man, do you mind to thank God for your wife ? What would become of you just now without her ? "

And David, who had taken all his wife's ministration as a matter of course, saw, for the first time for many a day, the tiredness of her face, and because he was not at heart a bad man, but merely a self-centred, careless one, he saw it now with pained surprise.

" You're no' tired, Mary, are you ? " he asked.

" No, no, Davy," she assured him.

" Oh, these wives," the Doctor said, " they're

hopeless ! She hasn't been in bed for six weeks, but she's not tired !" Words evidently failed him. He left behind him, as he always did, peace and harmony, and in the tender light on Mary's face he could read the dawning of a new and a happier day for the folks of the Haugh.

VIII

One more visit and he must retrace his footsteps. The Doctor was physically and mentally tired, yet at the thought of the last visit his face brightened. Angus Mackay was a Highlander and had the strange mystic seer spirit which belongs to certain Celts. For years blindness had been creeping on the old man, but as his bodily eyes failed him the eyes of his spirit grew keener and ever keener.

"You are welcome, sir," he said, going to the door ere the Doctor knocked ; "I knew your step."

He led the way into the spotless little kitchen where Merran, his wife, was busy at the baking of bannocks. "What a good smell," the Doctor said, giving an appreciative sniff. "Merran, a ' piece,' please, and a small bit of cheese."

"And what have you been doing to-day ? " the Doctor asked as he munched the crisp brown cakes and washed them down with a glass of new milk.

Angus smiled a little wistfully. "And what is there that a poor, blind, old man like me can be doing, but thinking, and thinking ? "

"What were you thinking about, Angus ? Merran, may I take another cake ? "

"Well, sir, if you had the Gaelic, or I had the right English, I could be telling you."

" Go on," said the Doctor. " You needn't always be casting up my ignorance."

" God forbid," Angus said, with so much simple earnestness, the Doctor burst out laughing.

" Well, sir, I was thinking about the disciples, and how the Lord was asking them one day, ' Whom do men say that I am ? ' Fine did they know that some were saying, ' He is a Samaritan ; He is a friend of publicans and sinners ; He has a devil ; He is mad '—and the Lord knew that too. But the disciples did not tell Him that. No, no. They said, ' Some say Thou art Elias ; some Jeremias ; some a great prophet ' ; but as for themselves they knew very well that He was greater than all the prophets—He was the Christ. It was because they loved Him so much they were so wise."

The Doctor, thinking of his encounter with Burnbraes that very day, laughed a little. " Aye, Angus, if we love we will bring to the loved one only what is likely to cheer him. It must have been a great day in the Master's life when Peter said ' Thou art the Christ.' "

IX

The sun was setting behind the distant Ben Wyvis as the Doctor walked homeward through a land drenched in silence. From far away, remote, forlorn, and undomestic, came the cry of the curlews, while circling over his head in troubled flight a pair of lap-wings flew with querulous, complaining voices. Those night sounds seemed to add to the lonesomeness of the night. To the Doctor the death of a summer day was always depressing. When he reached home he sat down wearily in his study chair, and found himseli longing like a sick bairn for the gladsome morning, and the stir of life awakening up to a new glad day.

Presently his housekeeper brought him the news that old Donald Forsyth had passed away, and though he expected it, yet he felt an added weight on his spirit. Long he sat brooding over the happenings of the day and the tidings which had come at the end of it. He leaned back wearily and closed his eyes. Deep sleep came to him, and then he saw to his surprise that he was standing outside a door along with a crowd of others. Soon a little group of bare-headed men carried out a coffin, and he saw the name " Donald Forsyth," and his age in stark, white letters on the lid. The outward trappings of death had always pained him, and he shuddered as he looked. Then from out of the grim black coffin there fell a mass of corruption, unspeakable, and loathsome ; but even as he sickened at the sight, lo ! emerging triumphant from the rottenness, there rose a form—young, raidant, fair, and lovely In ringing tones this shining one burst forth, " Ah, I knew that I would rise again ! " In a moment earth and the things of earth had passed, and there stood the Holy City, with the ransomed of the Lord gathered home, and he heard a song of matchless music, " Worthy is the Lamb, for Thou wast slain and hast redeemed us to God by Thy blood."

THE KING'S MESSENGER

IT was on a lovely Friday morning in June that Dr. Lindsay set out on a pilgrimage which had for its object the helping of a fellow-minister through his Highland Communion. Part of the journey was by rail ; part by the mail-coach. As the Doctor stepped out of the train and made his way to this latter, he stopped to sniff appreciatively the smell of peat-reek rising in lazy, blue clouds from the chimney of a little thatched cottage. Some starlings clustered and chattered on the roof of the station house, and lent an every-day note to a scene otherwise remote and solitary. From far-off hills echoed the lonely cry of the curlew, lapwings complained (quite untruthfully) that someone was robbing their nests, and the larks, always joyous, filled the air with pulsing melody.

Rory, the mail-driver, hoisted the Doctor's bag into the coach. This was followed by two sacks of mails, a hamper of bread, sundry small parcels, and, if one might trust one's nose, a box of kippered herrings.

" Now, sir," quoth Rory, " where would you like to sit—in the body or on the box ? "

In the " body " was already seated one passenger. After a quick glance at him, the Doctor chose the box, whereupon the passenger snorted and put his legs upon the seat. He had a squat, pump-like figure, a face round as a moon and sphinx-like in expression, eyes which were not neighbours, and a foolish-looking nose. His mouth was hidden behind a forest of red whiskers. His luggage consisted of a basket and an umbrella—the latter a most lady-like affair with a waist. He was clad in a suit of " blacks " made at some prehistoric date, when he too, had had a waist.

Rory addressed him as " Maister Mactougall," and inquired genially after his health.

"I canna complain," he replied cautiously, in a foggy tone of voice.

"Gran' day, sir," Rory began conversationally to the Doctor, climbing into his seat and gathering up the reins.

Next minute he gave an angry roar. "Weel, what now? We'll no' get started this side o' Christmas, I'm thinking!" This speech was hurled angrily at the stationmaster, who came hurrying out, carrying a huge bandbox. Rory's rage was of no moment to him. "Don't be forgetting the lassies' hats," he panted cheerily, "an' Donal the drover is asking, if you see a cattle beast on the road to let him know. Ye can tell the keeper, too, that yon ferret he sent to the Lodge is lost, an' he'd better send east another."

"Aye, aye," Rory grunted. "Ye can pit the box in beside Maister Mactougall. Any more orders?" he inquired with ominous politeness.

"No' that I can mind o'," the other replied blandly. "Good day, Rory!"

"You seem to get a lot of queer errands," chuckled the Doctor, who had been listening with keenest relish to the conversation.

Rory laughed too. "Allow me! From the penny 'purn' to a suit o' Sabbath-day 'blacks' an' a funeral hat, there's nothing but I get! *I once bought a dolman* for a wife up the Glen! I did that. You'll have heard o' dolmans, sir?"

The Doctor looked wise and nodded.

"There was another aaful thing the weemen was wearing aboot the same time—'*garrybaldies*' they was calling them. I refused to buy them for anyone, though as a rule I'm no' a blate man. I would not need to be!"

The Doctor looked wiser than ever, but no rash word escaped his lips. The subject scared him worse than it did the bold Rory.

Oh, the sweetness of the hill air as they journeyed on! Dr. Lindsay revelled in the sights and sounds and

gracious influences of the day. Rory, finding him even
thus early in his acquaintance a man after his own
heart, poured out story after story of interest. There
was the cairn where the tinker in the year eighteen
hundred and ever-so-few perished in a snowstorm ;
farther on was a big iron-clamped stone where a witch
had been burned ; yonder was the ruin of a castle
called, to begin with, Blackhall, but after a wild fight
with a cateran clan, changed to Castle Rhuig (Red),
and you can guess what the *red* was. Then there was
the ford of the Kelpies, weirdest of all places, for there
one might see that—

> " Knee deep she waded in the burn,
>> The Banshee robed in green,
>> She sang yon song the whole night long,
>> And washed the linen clean.
>> The linen that would wrap the dead,
>> She beetled on a stone,
>> She stood with dripping hands blood-red,
>> Low singing all alone,
> ' The linen robes are pure and white
>> For Fergus Mhor must die to-night.' "

" Man, that's fine," the Doctor said warmly, when
Rory had finished, and not without dramatic power
(for Rory was a Celt !) what is surely one of the eeriest
of Gaelic poems.

A hollow groan from the " body " made the others
aware that their fellow-traveller did not share these
sentiments.

" Are ye no' feeling aaful weel ? " Rory inquired
kindly. " Maybe sitting with all that o' weemen's hats
is no' agreeing with you ? "

There was no reply to this sally, and, looking at
Rory's face the Doctor was surprised to see the twinkle
die out of his eyes and an angry frown pucker his
forehead. He muttered something angrily below his
breath and made a (comparatively speaking, for his was

the kindest of hearts) wild lunge at the off-horse's flank.

"Haud up, there, lad!" he bawled angrily to the astonished horse. "It's a fine day, Kirsty," this last to a woman who was walking a little ahead of the coach.

The woman turned and looked meekly at the driver, as she wiped, not without ostentation, the moisture from her brow. "It is a fine day, as you say, Rory, but aaful warrum. You'll no' be feeling it up there, but if you wass walking! The sun fair takes the heart out o' my legs. Yet see you how disappointed I would be if I did not get west to the church!"

Rory sighed resignedly. "You'll better be coming up here then, and be keeping company to Maister Mactougall."

Very promptly did Kirsty avail herself of this none-too-gracious invitation. "May the Lord reward you, for I cannot," she said. Having thus got rid of all financial responsibility, she settled herself to have a talk with her fellow-traveller. Rory snorted and made a certain dark allusion to folks who were so mean that they would skin the very—but I had better not finish the sentence; Rory was a homely soul!

From Mr. Macdougall, now, Kirsty received a welcome that was almost enthusiastic. His one eye beamed —if there was a certain sternness in the other, it was certainly not for Kirsty.

"Wass you going to the sacrament?" he inquired in his peculiar foghorn tone of voice.

"I wass indeed," Kirsty replied. "I wass there on the Fast day too."

"And what sort of diet did you get? Wass it edifying?"

"Is that what you're saying?" Kirsty cried shrilly.

"You would be understanding him?"

Again Kirsty could only shrilly echo the question, adding piously, "The Lord forbid that I would be understanding the decent gentleman!"

Rory looked at the Doctor's face, then both men

looked hastily away at some distant object, and Rory remarked, apropos of nothing in particular, " Allow the weemen, just you allow them ! They're the boys ! "

" And where wass you, Maister Macdougall, since a long time ? There's a very long time since I didn't see you."

" I was away at Portree."

" At Portree ! Think of that now ! At a sacrament ! "

Mr. Macdougall nodded. " What other, Kirsty ? "

" And who wass you staying wiss—if it's not bad mainners to be asking ? "

" I wass staying wiss Mistress Macleod."

" Doesn't myself know her very well ! "

" A fine woman," cried Macdougall, " a fine, fine woman ! "

" She would be showing kindness to the stranger ? " Kirsty hazarded shrewdly. This worthy " stranger " waggled his head—words were utterly useless, at least English words, for the rest of the conversation was carried on in an undertone and in the Gaelic language.

" What sort of a day did you haff on the Friday ? " Kirsty inquired in her best " company " voice, perhaps feeling uneasy over what a Highlander always regards as a lapse of good manners.

" Grand ! " replied Macdougall. " There's yonder o' men the minister can lift, as many as five-and-twenty ! "

Kirsty rocked herself ; whether in admiration or envy one cannot tell.

Not unnaturally the Doctor was puzzled to hear of a minister whose merits seemed to outshine those of a circus acrobat. Rory, however, explained, in a whisper, that what he meant was that on the " Men's Day " or Friday, some question in theology is discussed by the men ; in this particular case there were twenty-five men willing (if not able) to take part in the discussion.

They were now fast approaching a brae, and Rory,

with almost unnecessary briskness, ordered his passengers in the " body " to alight.

" Keep your seat, sir," he said to the Doctor, in whom long ago he had recognised a kin spirit. Dr. Lindsay, however, would not hear of this favour, and descended with the others. He and Rory trudged on, slightly ahead, the Doctor humming softly, " Hold the fort," and seeming to derive much satisfaction from the verse which begins with " See the mighty host advancing ! "

Whether this apparently innocent melody had anything to do with Mr. Macdougall's decision to take a short cut over the hill, it is not for the historian to say. The fact remains that both he and Kirsty somewhat hastily took their departure—and " Thanking you kindly for your lift," this last from Kirsty.

" That'll no' do much to feed my horses," Rory remarked as they passed out of earshot. " Aye, sir, they're going to Clachan. Gorry Glen is a good bittie farther west. Ye can get up tae your seat again."

The next stopping place was Gorrybeg, and here Rory handed out his first mail-bag to the little, timid-looking woman waiting for it.

" Hoo's the coo ? " he inquired genially. " Yes, oh yes, I have the salts for her. Don't be giving her a too big dose an' keep her off the new grass for a while. A parcel ? What kind of a parcel, Mistress Macpherson ? "

" It was a bittie o' beef I was getting from Mackay the butcher in the town," she explained artlessly.

" Mackay the butcher, said ye ? " cried Rory, diving into all sorts of keeping places. " Would you, sir, be so good as to haud the reins till I have a look for this parcel ? Wait a wee now ; here's something, from Mackay, too ! Is that it ? No, no, that's a pair of cork soles from Mackay the shoemaker, for that wife at the toll house, her wi' the ' *romantic fivir* '—that's no' it. Cork soles would no' be as good as a beefsteak, though indeed the last beef I got mysell was as teuch (tough) as any cork soles. Would it be a big parcel ? "

" Jist a pound of boiling beef, Rory," the gentle little voice said, and suddenly it struck the Doctor that Rory was not in any particular hurry to find the parcel.

" Try your pockets," he suggested, with a twinkle in his eye.

Rory did.

" Weel, weel ! " he exclaimed, " am I no the amadan (fool) ? In ma pooch all the time ! Here you are, Mistress Macpherson. No, no, it's no bother in the world. How I forgot to look in ma pooch is more than I can think ! " Thus with amazing artfulness did the gallant Rory put by the time with little Mistress Mary Macpherson, Postmistress of Gorrybeg !

There was a certain constraint in his manner as they took the road again, but though perhaps the Doctor had glimpsed Rory's love-tale, there was nothing but warmest interest in his manner as he listened to the story.

" There was a time, sir, when she hadna a puckle meal in the house. I'm that glad she can buy beef now an' then."

" Aye," said the Doctor sympathetically. His manner invited confidences.

Rory nodded.

" Her man died, a poor feckless body at the best ; he went and died at the beginning o' harvest, leaving her with nothing between her an' the poors' hoose, but the coo, an' even she was dry ! An' little Sandy, her boyan, was just getting better o' whooping cough."

He paused as if considering the perversity of a man who would choose to die at such an inopportune time. " The coo was dry, as I said, an' hardly a blade o' grass left ; you'll mind o' the summer o' drought we had five-six years ago ? Weel, it came to be that poor Mary had neither bite nor sup in her hoose one morning, and the craiter was like to give up in despair. ' You'll be going to the hill with the coo,' says she to the child, ' An' will I be getting my breakfast when I came back ? ' says he, an' poor Mary had to let on she was not hearing

him. Weel, Sandy went off with the coo, an' Mary she's
to her knees. Have you the Gaelic, sir? No? Weel,
weel, it's all the same. When she came to the place
where you say, ' *Tabhair an dhuinn n-aran laitheil*,' in
the English that means, ' Give us this day our daily
bread,' wasn't there a chap (knock) at the door. And
who was this but big Donald, the keeper from the top of
the Glen! An' says he, ' How are you the day, Mistress Macpherson, an' will you be so good as to give
me a drink of water? An' if you would please to
throw this packet of sangwidges to your hens, an' empty
the tea out of this flask, I would be aaful obleeged.
You see, I'm going up the hill with the shooting gents,
an' they always take so much meat with them, I'm
wearied carrying it.' Aye, an' when the little fellow
came home from the hill it was the fine breakfast his
mother had waiting on him ! "

The Doctor's eyes were bright with sympathy. " He
is faithful that promised," he said softly.

" Aye, an' more than that," Rory went on. " Donald
the keeper spoke to His Grace aboot Mary, an' he gave
her the Post Office an' a free hoose an' grazing for her
coo, an' now she's able to buy her beef an' all her orders
an' to send Sandy in his new kilt to the school with the
other bairns."

The Doctor seemed to be turning something over in
his mind. " You're a married man? " he inquired.

Rory's face was always red, but it seemed to become
a trifle redder as he stammered, " N-n-no, sir."

" Too young? " the Doctor inquired wickedly.

Rory gave a great roar of laughter. " No, sir ; but—
but—jist aaful blate ! "

And what followed after that is a secret, which only
the Doctor, Rory, and one other person know.

. . . .

The welcome Dr. Lindsay got was rapturous when
he reached his journey's end. The minister's wife had
belonged to his congregation in her girlhood's days ;

indeed it was partly for her sake he had undertaken this long journey.

"Why, Katherine, is this you?" he cried as she came hurrying down the garden path to meet him.

"And who else could it be?" she asked gaily.

"*I thought it was a lady*," he replied solemnly (but his eyes twinkled !).

"That's because I put on my best frock in your honour," she assured him, and then they both began to laugh. The sight of his face, the sound of his voice, and the old delightsome banter unlocked such floods of fond, glad recollections that if she had not laughed, then she would certainly have cried.

"Are you very tired?" she inquired presently. "You must go straight to bed, whenever you have had dinner."

"I won't," he replied firmly. "I won't be put to bed like a bad baby because, forsooth, you have a house of your own. Impudence! Where's that boy of yours?"

Before she could answer, a little boy of about four years came marching to meet them. He advanced bravely, a sturdy, untidy little figure in a ragged kilt, and clutching in a grubby small fist a certain culinary utensil known to Kate-of-the-kitchen as the "tattie chapper." Within a few feet of the Doctor he stood stock still, earnestly scrutinising the old minister's face, then, flinging aside what was presumably his club, this primitive man advanced with beaming face and outstretched hand.

"Peta 'ikes 'oo," he announced.

"And I like Peter," replied the Doctor promptly, for it is thus, with simple directness, deep calleth unto deep!

"Katherine, please, my bag. Do you like elephants, Peter?"

"The kind God makes?" the child asked. "Meat ones?"

The Doctor's face fell.

" Come, now, Peter, be reasonable. You wouldn't expect a little baggie like this to hold a real meat elephant. Watch what happens when his head comes off."

Behold, when the obliging beast was decapitated, his interior was stuffed full of sweeties ! A very prince of elephants !

" And where's Himsell ? " the Doctor asked when he could spare a minute from Peter. " And is dinner nearly ready ? I'm famished. If you don't give me something to eat I shall have to begin with ' *boy* ' and end with ' *elephant*,' eh, Peter ? "

But just as Mrs. Mackenzie was explaining that this was the " Men's Day," and that they would not wait for Himsell, the door opened to admit the minister.

" Surely you could not have had five-and-twenty men to lift like the stalwart of Portree ! " the Doctor laughed, and then he related what he had heard in the mail-coach. The meal was a merry one, and the younger minister, who had been feeling his spirit somewhat chafed with all the worries of a Highland Communion, presently found himself wondering why, in all the world, he had been fretting over what were trifles. He " smiled to think God's greatness flowed around our incompleteness ; round our restlessness His rest." That was because the Doctor sat at his table, and from before his presence all nagging, rasping irritations vanished.

In spite of lusty protestations, he was bundled off to the study couch to rest till tea-time, and Peter, with Jumbo in his arms, went about on tip-toe, making the most elaborate attempts at walking quietly that were ever beheld.

.   .   .   .

On Saturday, Dr. Lindsay, just to assert his independence, insisted upon accompanying Mr. Mackenzie to the Gaelic service in the evening. It was followed by a distribution of " tokens," and a meeting of the kirk session.

"Will David Macintyre be coming forward?" the Doctor heard one elder ask, and because the question was in English he found himself listening for the reply. In some occult fashion, he sensed a tragedy behind the words, and though the reply came in Gaelic, he knew it was unfavourable. William Sutherland, the elder, a man who had continually lamented the present-day depravity, though he did nothing to improve it, sighed dismally and shook his head.

"Backslider!" he groaned.

The Doctor's generous heart was immediately on the side of the absent backslider. His rich and varied experience in church work had taught him the importance of prayer and patience, but before he could utter a word Mr. Mackenzie came up to him. In a low voice he said, "I fear this meeting is likely to last for some time. We have a case of church discipline before us. Would you mind going into Donald the catechist's house and waiting for me? He is a saint; you'll enjoy a talk with him. I'll call for you whenever we are through. Just open the door and go straight in. He is ill, unfortunately, otherwise he would be here to-night. You remember how we came from the Manse? Well, instead of going all that way, turn to the right at the cross-roads; you can't miss it."

The Doctor took his hat and his departure, just pausing at the door to say, as if thinking aloud, "Charity suffereth long, and is kind." William Sutherland, righteous-over-much, scowled evilly to himself.

The evening air felt like a benediction after the heated atmosphere of the meeting-place. The setting sun was filling the strath with glory. The Doctor paused at the cross-roads to ask himself, "Did he say the left hand or the right?" Because the left-hand one went the way of the setting sun, he chose it. Presently he found himself in front of what was unmistakably a carpenter's shop and house. Remembering the instructions, he lifted the "sneck" of the house door and entered.

"Who's there?" cried a gruff voice.

"A messenger of the King," promptly replied the Doctor, making his way into the kitchen. The owner of the gruff voice was sitting by the fire and eyed him in no friendly fashion. His wife, busy at her baking board, became so flurried she began to knead her bannocks "widdershins" instead of "deasoil"—that is, against the sun instead of with it—a forbidden ritual in the baking of bread! Yet there was nothing in the presence of the kindly stranger to cause any uneasiness.

"Mr. Mackenzie told me to wait here till he would join me," he explained, looking for some place to put his hat. The woman came forward timidly, placed a chair for him, and took possession of hat and stick.

"And how are you?" the Doctor asked genially of the dark-browed man. "I am glad to see you are able to be out of bed. Your minister told me you were bedridden."

"I might be in my bed or in my grave for all that him or any of his elders care," the man said sullenly. The Doctor was puzzled by his reception, but if you think he was daunted, then you don't know Dr. Lindsay in the least. Quite clearly he had come to the wrong house, yet it was not the wrong house either, for here was a man imprisoned in a bond of bitterness, and the Father had sent him to set the prisoner free. With a quick prayer for guidance, the King's messenger sat down and spread out his hands to the blaze.

"Do you know, I'm quite glad to see a fire, though it is the month of June," he began conversationally. "I haven't seen a peat fire like this since I was a bairn going for holidays to my granny's in Strath Dorran. I can remember yet the taste of the bannocks toasted in front of——"

"Strath Dorran!" the man interrupted with great excitement, and in a flash the Doctor knew that his prayer for guidance had been answered, and that the Father had put into his hand the key of this man's prison house. With another swift prayer for further guidance, he turned to meet the man's questioning eyes. Like grey ghosts at cock-crow, all the bitter thoughts with which the house had been peopled fled and the atmosphere became at once peaceable and friendly.

" Div ye ken Strath Dorran ? " the man asked, and his speech was the speech of a Lowlander.

" My granny lived there. I used to go there every summer for holidays."

" Ye—ye'll no' be ony freen tae auld Mrs. Begg of Inverdorran ? " the man whispered fearfully.

" I'm her grandson," the Doctor nodded, smiling.

" It cowes a'," the man said, still speaking in the same fearful voice. " Div' ye mind on David Macintyre the vricht (wright) ? "

" Don't I ? " the Doctor chuckled. " He gave me my first boat—a beauty it was too !—called ' The Running Rill.' "

The man gave a little sigh, whether of pleasure or of pain who shall say, for are they not twin-brothers ?

" He was my father," he said slowly and simply. Words, after all, are unhelpful things at moments of great crisis. The two men shook hands, their faces shining.

Then followed a flood of reminiscence and question. It was " Do you mind the Dorran Burn ? And where's your brother Jamie ? Wasn't he the loon for the trout ? And where's Helen, your sister ? I mind how she could climb trees. And what's your name ? I think I remember you, though you cannot mind me—you were a baby in frockies then ! "

When had the kitchen rung with such happy laughter before ? Even Jean, the shy wife (because she had not the good English) found herself joining in it, as she softly laid a meal on the table.

" But what's your name ? " the Doctor repeated.

" I'm David, sir ; called after ma faither."

David Macintyre ; where had the Doctor heard the name before ? Like a flash there broke in on his remembrance the scene in the meeting-house, and the cruel, relentless face of old William Sutherland. Clearly the Father had guided him here. " I will bring the blind by a way that they know not," he thought.

" Tell me, then, Davy, how it came to pass that you are living here ? " For a moment the man's face clouded, as he explained how, by a series of strange happenings, he had married a glen-woman, and had settled down in her father's business as a carpenter. He had been a lonely man, for even the speech of the glen folks had been to him a hidden thing, and as for the workings of their minds, that he had never even faintly comprehended. Yet all this could have been borne if the little son who had came to them when they were both somewhat late in life had been spared. " He was only seven, when "—he paused and choked—

" When he went home," the Doctor said.

There was a tense silence for a few minutes, and then, like a burn in spate, out came the flood of bitterness which had been gathering in the heart of David Macintyre for six long, weary years.

His sorrow for his child—his one and only son—was great, and what sorrow is there like it in all the world ? The old minister had died ; Mr. Mackenzie had not come, and William Sutherland, the elder, had taken it upon himself to visit the bereaved couple. With many groans and moans William had asked them what evidence had they that their child was one of the elect ? They would like to think, no doubt, that he was, but how could they tell ? At first the stricken father did not comprehend what William was driving at, then the elder quoted, " ' Whom He did foreknow He also did predestinate ; whom He did predestinate He also called.' Read your Bible, David Macintyre, and don't take it upon yourself to say you'll see your child again."

" The wife there fented," David said drily, " and I put the elder oot o' the door, an' I said—" he paused, his throat working convulsively.

" Aye, aye," said the Doctor musing aloud and

affecting not to see David's emotion. "And one shall say unto Him, 'What are those wounds in Thine hands?' Then He shall answer, '*Those with which I was wounded in the house of My friends.*' You surely didn't believe that the Heavenly Father would do what no earthly father would do?"

"It's this doctrine of election," David groaned. "If wee Davy is no' one of the elect, then I'm no' seekin' to gang to heaven. I wadna be nane contentit."

"Oh, hush, hush, man!" his wife said in a fright.

"An' I'll no hush then!" he stormed. "For sax years I've been like a man in prison, ma heid tellin' me ae thing an' ma hert the tither. Oh, sir, tell me the richts o't!" It was a sore cry wrung from the throbbing centre of the man's heart.

"Poor soul!" the Doctor said pitifully. "Oh, Davy, do you not understand that election is the rock on which we stand—not, thank God! the door by which we enter. You understand that, don't you? Why, in the days of His flesh, there were some who would keep back the bairns from the Lord. They didn't call it the doctrine of election, they said it was troubling the Master. What He said then is what He says now and always, 'Suffer the children to come unto Me, and forbid them not.'"

The man's face was knit with agony, yet as he listened to the gracious words of the King's messenger a softer expression crept into his haggard eyes.

The Doctor's memory was always a source of pride to us, and now, very softly and very perfectly, he repeated :—

THE MAISTER AN' THE BAIRNS [1]

The Maister sat in a wee cot hoose,
  Tae the Jordan's waters near ;
An' the fisher fowk crushed an' croodit roon',
  The Maister's words tae hear.

[1] This little poem was written by William Thomson, born in Glasgow, 1860, died 1883.

An' even the bairns frae the near-haun' streets
  War mixin' wi' the thrang,
Laddies an' lassies wi' wee bare feet
  Jinkin' the crood amang.

An' ane o' the Twal' at the Maister's side
  Rase up an' cried alood—
" Come, come, bairns, this is nae place for you,
  Rin awa hame oot o' the crood."

But the Maister said, as they turned awa',
  " Let the wee bairns come tae Me ! "
An' He gaithered them roon' Him whar He sat,
  An' liftit ane up on His knee—

Ay, He gaithered them roon' Him whar He sat,
  An' straikit their curly hair ;
An' He said tae the won'erin' fisher fowk
  That croodit aroon' Him there :—

" Sen'na the weans awa frae Me,
  But raither this lesson learn,
That nane'll win in at Heaven's yett,
  That isna as pure as a bairn ! "

An' He that wisna' oor kith an' kin,
  But a Prince of the Far-awa',
Gaithered the wee anes in His airms,
  An' blessed them ane an' a'.

·　　·　　·　　·　　·　　·　　·

O Thou Who watchest the ways o' men,
  Keep our feet in the heavenly airt,
An' bring us at last tae Thy hame abune
  As pure as the bairns in he'rt.

Of what followed we may not here speak, but when
at last the Doctor rose to go, he left behind him the
peace of God.

" I'll be looking for you to-morrow, both of you, at

the Table," he said. " Well, David, you may come and give me a Scotch convoy."

Meantime in the Manse there was a great anxiety as to what had become of the Doctor. When Mr. Mackenzie had called at the catechist's house, it was to be told that the Doctor had not called there at all. Concluding that he had gone straight home, the minister followed, only to be told that the Doctor had not returned.

The session meeting had been a long and trying one for Mr. Mackenzie. Some of the elders, more eager for the letter of the law than for the salvation of souls, had urged that the communion roll be purged of the names of David Macintyre and his wife Jean, who had absented themselves from the means of grace for six years, without giving any reason. After a veritable Waterloo, it had been arranged that the minister, for whom little things of this sort are invariably reserved, should call upon the erring ones and reason with them. Frankly speaking, the prospect did not attract the minister, to whom David Macintyre had ever shown his most distant and repellant manner. He had had visions of asking his wise old friend to accompany him on this difficult mission. Judge, then, of his surprise when, in going forth to look for the Doctor, he beheld him coming strolling along the road in deep and intimate conversation with the very man whose case was causing him so much anxiety. At the foot of the garden they parted, after a warm handshake, and took their separate ways. The Doctor was humming softly to himself, " He comes the prisoners to release."

.   .   .   .

A Highland Communion Sabbath is much more of a great " occasion " than a Lowland one. For one thing the services are double, so while Dr. Lindsay officiated in the church in English, Mr. Mackenzie took the Gaelic service in the meeting-house.

The day held a holy hush—it seemed as if even

Nature knew it was God's own day. From far and near the folks gathered. It is rather a pretty custom which requires that every woman shall have on her best and newest garments to do honour to the day, and that every man who possesses a black suit and a tall hat shall don the same on the Communion Sabbath. White shirts, too, are the order of the day, at once the pride and despair of their wearers (who have been known to go home with their stiff collars in their pockets, to the scandal of their women-folk and their own vast comfort).

. The little band of elders, all clad in their decent best blacks, sat beneath the pulpit, the solemn and sacred elements spread on a linen-covered table before them. A strange custom prevails of leaving the tables empty until the time comes to " serve " them. Then, with slow and reverent tread, the members come forward to " remember their Lord."

The Doctor preached, as only he could do, on the words, " *What think ye, that He will not come to the feast ?* " Very clearly he proved that He had come to this feast, that His presence filled the house on this His holy day. After a rapturous hour, he invited all those who loved their Lord to take their places at His table.

Whilst the members were coming forward, Angus the precentor chanted line after line of the 116th Psalm. " I love the Lord, because my voice," Angus sang in strange tuneful voice. " I love the Lord because my voice," the congregation echoed. So on line after line the sweet song was sung. The tables by this time were almost full. The Doctor had come down from the pulpit, and was standing among the elders.

" Yet there is room," he said, as the last note of the psalm died away. " We shall sing other four lines beginning at the words, ' I'll of salvation take the cup.' " Again the strange chant rang through the church. Angus had reached the words, " On God's name will I call," when a couple sitting near the door rose, and with downcast faces and beating hearts took the places they had left empty for six long years.

" I'll pay my vows now to the Lord," chanted Angus, and two new voices, rather tremulously, sang the words after him.

Something had moved the Doctor. He stood, a notable figure with his splendid reverence and dignity, and with a strangely uplifted expression on his face. A solemn hush filled the church. Women trembled, they knew not why, and men gripped their jaws lest they shame themselves. Then the Doctor's voice began to read, " For I have received of the Lord that which also I delivered unto you, how that the Lord Jesus the same night in which He was betrayed took bread," and so on through what is surely one of the most solemn and soul-searching chapters in the Bible. " With desire I have desired to eat this passover with you before I go hence," were the words of his " Table address."

In the prayer which followed the Unseen seemed very real, very near. Old Granny Bruce, the deafest woman in the parish, said afterwards, " I did not hear a word he said, but I knew the Lord did, *for He was nearer him than I was*, and I was in the front seat."

The sacred elements were now uncovered, and with reverent hand the Doctor handed them to the waiting elders. " This is My body broken for you. This cup is the new testament in My blood—this do, in remembrance of Me."

Slowly and carefully, down either aisle, the elders filed, bearing in their hands the vessels of the Lord. After all had been served, the Doctor, still standing among the elders, said a few words to help and sustain the members when the world and Monday morning should claim them again.

Like a great shout of triumph, and to the stirring notes of " Effingham," the last psalm was sung. " Oh thou, my soul, bless God the Lord." David Macintyre, moved and inspired, lifted his eyes from his book to

meet the understanding eyes of the Doctor, fixed upon
him.   Then he sang in his rich bass voice, and everyone
knows the rapture of the bass of Effingham :—

> " Who doth redeem thy life, that thou
>   To death may'st not go down."

    .   .   .   .

At night the church was crowded, a sight to gladden
and inspire any preacher, and when that preacher was
Dr. Lindsay, then you might prepare for a feast or a
" diet," to use the old expressive Scottish word.   His
text was, " He hath sent me . . . to preach deliverance
to the captives," and the love and fatherhood of God
were his theme.   Rory the mail-driver had walked six
miles to hear the minister to whom his heart had gone
out on Friday, but whose name, strange to say, he had
not heard.   Enthralled he listened, elbows on the book-
board and eyes fixed unwinkingly on the preacher's
face, afraid almost to breathe, lest he might lose a single
word.

The service past, like a man in a dream he went forth
to lie in wait for his crony, Dugald Macgregor, who had
been wont to boast most outrageously about a certain
minister he had once heard.

" Man, yon's preaching for you ! "   Rory exulted.
" I knew he could do it !   Ach man, if that minister
you're always blowing about could preach like him we
heard the night, then you might well mention it."

Dugald listened with the utmost patience, and then,
with a sly twinkle in his eye, he said coolly, " Yon *iss*
the minister I'm always blowing about, and can ye
blame me ?   Yon, then, Rory, is Dr. Lindsay for you ! "

In the house of David Macintyre the Doctor was
saying a few words of farewell.   He was accompanied
by—William Sutherland !   It was not to the house of
David Macintyre alone that the King's messenger had
brought liberty on this memorable Sabbath day.

" Last night, David," the Doctor said, and his face

was rapt, " I had an audience of the King, whose messenger I am. I told Him about you, David, and I prayed that He might come to the feast to-day. As I spoke with Him I noticed that standing close beside Him, clinging to His hand, was a little boy—yes, just such a little boy as that." He nodded towards a little faded portrait hanging over the mantelpiece.

Jean Macintyre, her face working piteously, uttered a little sob. " Oh, Davy, Davy voch (little) ! " she whispered passionately.

" Ay, it was just Davy," the Doctor went on. " ' This little boy is rather lonely,' the Lord said to me, ' for six years he had been coming with Me to My feast at Gorry Glen, hoping to see his father and mother there.' "

David Macintyre, with set jaw, got up suddenly from his seat by the fire, and faced the window. There is something awesome in the grief of a strong man, and for a few tense seconds no one spoke, it seemed as if no one dared to breathe.

Presently the Doctor's voice went on softly ; " ' You'll meet them to-morrow,' I said. The bairn was glad, and the Lord said, ' It's what Davy and Myself have been waiting for.' " The Doctor's voice sank to a whisper. " And I saw them both at His Table to-day."

David Macintyre suddenly turned round from the window, and his face was the face of a man who has glimpsed some heavenly vision of which it is not lawful to speak.

" I—I thought I saw Davy, too," he whispered slowly. " It was that time when you said, ' Yet there is room,' and Jean and masell came forward."

The Doctor nodded. " He was there, with the Lord, just as he'll be there, with the Lord, when we gather into the feast above. Here, we see but as in a glass—darkly ; but—there,—face—to—face ! "

DAVY'S DOG

LITTLE DAVY, the minister's five-year-old boy, lay ill. Folks said (though not to his mother) that the child was dying. For ten long days now he had lain in the grip of some mysterious childish ailment. A racing pulse, a soaring temperature told of the enemy which was eating away the boy's slender reserves of strength. Sometimes he would rave and toss about wildly, spending with the prodigality of delirium the strength he needed to fight his illness. Then again, spent and wan-faced, he would lie back on his pillow with closed eyes. At such times it seemed to his anguished mother that Davy's soul was adventuring forth into uncharted seas, whither his mother could not follow—whence he himself might never return.

" Speak to me, Davy," she pleaded in a whisper.

But the child never stirred ; his blue-veined eyelids might have veiled dead eyes, so little sign of life was there.

He remained like that all the evening. The doctor thought that possibly to-night the crisis of the illness might come. " If we can keep down his temperature and get him to sleep, Mrs. Sutherland, I think we 'll pull him through," he had said.

He had left mother and son about eight o'clock. Now it was growing late, and still Davy seemed to be in a semi-conscious state.

Then, about midnight, he began to toss and to mutter to himself. When he opened his eyes there was no gleam of recognition in them, and all at once a wave of desolation and loneliness broke over his mother's heart. Up till now she had been, outwardly at least, brave. But to-night—to-night there was no courage left in the heart of her. It had been raining all the evening, with the steady persistence which one sometimes sees in a June evening. Perhaps that was depressing her.

Then her husband was away doing chaplain duty in a southern port. Kind neighbours had offered to come and sit with the sick child, but she would not hear of this, and now suddenly she wished there was someone with her to share this anxious vigil.

Dr. Lindsay had come to take her husband's place. What he was to her during those dark days, only those who knew the Doctor in their day of trouble can realise. Still, he was an old man, and she hesitated about disturbing him.

There was something awesome in being the only person awake in a sleeping house, and unconsciously, as time went slowly past, her movements became more noiseless, her voice more of a whisper.

" Drink this, Davy, my lammie ! " She held a spoon to his lips.

With an impatient fling of his arm the child sent spoon and glass flying with a crash against the table.

" Davy wants his Davy's dog," he said suddenly. " Please, please."

" Yes, darling," she whispered bravely. " Take this to please mammy first. Davy mustn't make a noise. You'll waken Dr. Lindsay."

" Davy wants his Davy's dog," the little voice insisted. And then he began to cry and wring his hands. It was agony to see him wasting his strength, but the mother was faced with a problem which was insoluble. Just then Dr. Lindsay stole softly into the room.

" No, the noise did not waken me," he assured her ; " I was not sleeping. I want to know how you are now, David," he said, laying upon the child's hot, restless, little hands his own cool one.

The child stopped his distressing crying and whispered : " Please, I want my Davy's dog—now—this instant moment." The little voice was shrill by the end of the request.

His mother went to the window and stood looking into the dark night. She could see in her mind's eye the little green mound beneath the apple tree, where

Davy's dog had been buried. The very day the child had fallen ill, the dog he loved so well had been killed by a passing motor lorry. He had been Davy's inseparable companion, when—the one a baby, and the other a puppy—they had rolled about and played unending games in the garden. It seemed to her in her present mood an ominous and a dreadful thing that Davy's dog should have left his little master. There was no dog like Davy's dog, a lovely sable collie with a white ruff about his neck, and a tail as feathery as an ostrich plume. And now the child was calling for the dog. If he were not satisfied, she knew the consequences would be fatal. " The child must be kept quiet," she had been told. It was a cruel thing that in the hour of crisis Davy should have set his heart upon what was so hopelessly impossible.

" What shall we do ? " she asked, desperately turning to the old Doctor.

" Davy wants his Davy's dog," the persistent little voice wailed.

The mother took a photograph of a happy-faced, bare-legged laddie with his arm round the neck of a collie, and tried to put it into the child's hand.

" Here is the pretty picture of Davy and his dog," she said with attempted gaiety. " See, darling, the photograph we got taken for daddy."

The child thrust it away angrily.

" Davy wants his real dog," he said firmly.

As she replaced the picture on the mantel-shelf it seemed to mock her. That handsome dog—gone ! And the bonnie bairn—was he to go also ? Suddenly she hid the photograph behind the clock. It was unbearable.

Meanwhile the old Doctor was kneeling beside the bed, his face buried in his hands. The room became full of the voiceless currents of prayer—agonising prayer, for well did the old man know how critical was the situation.

When he looked up his face was calm and tranquil.

" My dear," he said in his fatherly way, " do you

think you could get me a cup of tea ? Yes, yes, of course, Kate gave me supper ; but that was long ago. Ages ago ! " He nodded towards the clock. " It'll soon be breakfast time ; it's half-past two. No, madam ! I won't go back to bed ! I want tea and toast." There was a twinkle in his eye as he added, " an egg too ! I'll call you if I think Davy needs you. *Don't come though, till I call.*"

Full well did the wise old man know that in occupation Mrs. Sutherland would find a little respite from her anxiety. Well did he know, too, that her Highland nature, with the instincts of hospitality inculcated in it from her earliest fore-folk, would express no astonishment at his request.

" I think I could eat two rounds of toast," he remarked blandly, and opened the door for her.

Outside the closed door she stood. Every nerve in her body was strained to listen. The little wailing voice rang out in a peculiarly forlorn fashion. " Davy wants his Davy's dog," again and again.

" God help us," she agonised. " Oh, God, help my bairn."

The rain was falling with steady monotony on the roof. It was the hour when Nature herself is at her feeblest. Night was busy with the article of death, and day had not been born. The mother shivered as she moved about the ghostly kitchen, where the old, everyday things seemed unfamiliar, unreal. She thought of one of Hans Andersen's fairy tales, where he tells how the kitchen utensils, when human beings are fast asleep, frolic and play and boast of their high birth to each other. She must remember to tell Davy about this when he was better ; he loved fairy tales. Listen, was that Davy calling ? Like a grey ghost she glided up the stairs. Davy was still wailing.

The Doctor had asked her to do a hard thing, she told herself. Why should he have sent her out of the room when Davy might be needing her ? Ah, but Davy did not need her ; that was the cruel part of it. It was for his dog he wailed. That was cruel. God was cruel. He had forgotten to be gracious. Her heart was bitter. Floods of black despair swept over her soul. Outside in " the dead unhappy night, the rain was on the roof."

Kate, the maid, had " rested " the peat fire, and with the tongs, always the most important fire-iron on a Highland hearth, Davy's mother set the peats on end and fanned them into a cheerful blaze. As she filled the kettle at the sink in the window, she heard a strange noise, almost like a distant rocket—not so loud as the big guns, yet having in it something sinister and uncanny. Just at the moment, too, the hall clock gave the peculiar " birr " with which it always gave warning of its intentions, and the strokes one—two—three ! rang out. Her first thought, of course, was of Davy. Had he heard the strange distant boom ? Had it frightened him ? She would just run up once more and see. But Davy's soul was wandering in places where no earthly sound could reach him. He was calling, calling, calling, the same pitiful wail.

Coming downstairs again, the mother saw through the uncurtained hall window, the one which looked towards the sea, that the searchlights were out. Their great golden swords crossed and uncrossed, piercing the gloom, sending now a shaft of light over the land, now flinging one into the lap of the sky. There was a great naval base on the other side of the firth, and the folks had grown used to hearing guns booming out at all sorts of hours ; to seeing searchlights flashing ; to seeing the restless battleships passing to and fro. Yet this night seemed, to the anxious watcher, to be full of strange influences. The powers of darkness were abroad, and were warring with the powers of light. She shivered as she crouched on the hearthstone, waiting for the kettle to boil.

II

It was the wheezy clock which wakened her. How awful ! She had been asleep for a whole hour ! Had the Doctor called ? Was—was—how was Davy ? For a minute or two she felt bewildered ; her mind refused to act. Davy—yes, it was not a dream ; Davy was ill upstairs and she had slept. Upstairs she flew, and stood listening once more. Silence deep, intense, restful, was there. Softly, as softly as the dawn was now stealing over the land, there was borne in on her the conviction that all was well with the child. She almost fancied she could hear his quiet breathing. It was hard to stay outside the door, yet the Doctor had made her promise not to come till he would call. How had the Shunammite woman passed the hours while another Man of God had taken her little son into his keeping ? Had she spent the night listening at the door ?

The rain had ceased. The world was bathed in tremulous, golden light. She opened the front door and let the blessed light in. The black night had flown—thank God. Nothing is so unbearable in the daytime as it is at night. From the drenched garden stole the fragrance of sweet briar and honeysuckle. Overhead a lark was singing with matchless melody ; from some distant farm town a cock greeted the sun with cheery briskness ; up from the sea came the tang of salt seaweed. And even as she stood by the door drinking in the sweet moist smells there pattered up the path a collie-dog—a sable collie with a white ruff round its neck, an ostrich feather for his tail !

In the half-open door he paused and looked in with the " please-may-I-come-in " expression which belongs to all polite collies. He was not Davy's dog certainly, but no two dogs could possibly be more alike.

" Come, doggie," she said, and held out her hand.

The animal, with his eyes full of friendliness, advanced with a smile and a wave of his tail.

Then, just then—for God never comes a minute too soon—she heard the noise she had been waiting for all night long, the sound of the opening door and of the Doctor's voice.

" Come, doggie, come along," she whispered, and both ran upstairs. " Is—is——" she panted, her eyes devouring the little face on the pillow.

" Did you bring Davy's dog ? " the child asked anxiously.

For answer she made him put his little wasted hand on the dog's head.

With a rapturous little sigh of supreme satisfaction he whispered, " *Davy's dog !* " That was all—but it was enough. There was a look of deepest content on the little face as he turned on his side and fell asleep, to sleep through the long hours which were to bridge the gulf between death and life.

And the old Doctor ? His face was the face of a man who had been on the mountain tops with God. Serene and happy were his eyes, but no ways surprised. The loving kindness of his Father was no new thing to him.

" It is the Lord's doing and it is marvellous in our eyes," he said softly.

Then with gracious words did he pour out his heart in prayer. Thus in the old time did the Man of God call an anxious mother and say, " *Thy son* "—" *and she fell at his feet and bowed herself to the ground.*"

As he was leaving the room, his task done, she looked up with a very April face to say :

" Your tea, Doctor ? It's all ready."

" Tea ! " he echoed with a twinkle in his eye. " I had forgotten. You take it, my dear. My meat is to do the will of Him that sent me."

And the explanation ? Marvellous, yet simple with the simplicity of all great things. The noise Davy's mother heard at three o'clock, which had sounded like a rocket, was the noise of an explosion on board the battleship, *Beltane Queen.* The public learned in due course that the captain stuck to his ship to the very last, and his constant companion, a sable collie, stayed, too. When a boat hurried to the rescue, the captain lifted his dog and threw him into it. " Get a good home for him *someone,*" he begged. But the faithful dog, madly struggling, plunged into the sea again and tried to rejoin his master. What became of him? Was he sucked under with the sinking vessel? Dr. Lindsay and Davy's mother have their own thoughts as they look at Davy, a tall, lanky, big-eyed Davy playing with a sable collie. "*The Lord's doing—and marvellous in our eyes.*"

THE DOCTOR "SUPPLIES"

THE lights burned low in the smoky station lamps. The Saturday crowd who awaited the arrival of the last train, shivered and shuddered in the keen east wind which blew in snell and pitiless from the sea, scarce a hundred yards beyond the station. The night was dark; and in the sky not a friendly star was to be seen.

"It'll be snow gin mornin'," an old fisherman prophesied; "that bank o' clouds to the nor'ard is snow, and that's the airt o' the win' the nicht!" As the folks peered through the darkness they saw at last the bright lights of the incoming train, and heard the engine lift up its voice in welcome if unmusical greeting. "At last," Mrs. Urquhart said to herself, with a sigh of relief.

The crowd of passengers descended from the train, and for a minute or two she found herself unable to get out of the spot. She looked anxiously along the row of open doors, but she did not see the stranger she had come to meet. Quickly she examined carriage after carriage, but in vain. No one the least resembling a minister was to be seen. Along in the outer darkness of the guard's van she heard a fisherwoman pouring out effusive thanks to some unseen person. "Thank you kindly, sir, I can manage fine now. It's no' too heavy—I've many's a time carried far mair," she was saying. Then as she passed out of the station, creel on back, Mrs. Urquhart noticed a tall figure looming behind, tying the flaps of his tweed cap underneath his chin. With a feeling of thankfulness, which only the dwellers in a Manse who are faced on a Saturday night with the problem of " no supply " can understand, she went to meet the welcome stranger.

"Dr. Lindsay?" she asked timidly.

"'Dr. Livingstone, I presume,'" answered the tall stranger, and the aptness of the repartee unlocked a flood of laughter. In the flickering lights she could see his eyes twinkling merrily. "And who are you?" he inquired. "You are not Stanley, are you?"

"No," she admitted; "I'm only the minister's wife, and I've come to meet you. Here's a boy who will carry your bag."

No one who has ever shaken hands with the old Doctor can forget the warmth and friendliness of that clasp. "You had no business to come out on such a night," he said severely. "Well, boy, you may carry my bag, but I can't allow anyone but myself to carry this." "This" was a white paper bag, which, judging by the careful way he carried it, must contain something precious. "How are your bairns?" he inquired suddenly.

"They are very well," she answered. "How clever of you to know I had bairns."

"You would wonder at the things I know," he replied with a waggish look. "Although we have never met before, I know lots of things about you. I know, for instance, that your husband is ill, and that's why I am 'supplying' for him. How is he?—or don't you say in the Highlands, 'How's himsell?'"

"Himsell's getting better," she answered gaily—the night had grown, she thought, much milder; "he's hoping to be home next month. How did you know I'm Highland?" she asked; "I thought I had no accent."

"I never met anyone yet who didn't pride themselves on having no accent," he chuckled. "'Thy speech bewrayeth thee!' Did you ever hear of the Captain of the steamer in which a famous Scotsman once crossed to New York? They were great friends, and as they were nearing Sandy Hook the Captain said, 'Weel, sir, I hope I'll hev the plaisure o' your company on the return voyage. Ye ken I come frae Scotland masel'; it wiss on the tip o' my tongue to tell ye, but I jest thocht I wad never lat on and then tak' ye by surprise!'"

The old Doctor's way of telling a story cannot be

reproduced in cold print. One had to hear him and to see him, too, to appreciate properly his art.

As they walked along he asked tenderly and sympathetically for the sick husband, and by the time the Manse was reached they felt as if they were old friends, for had not their acquaintance begun in the freemasonry of laughter, the surest and quickest of all paths to friendship.

" Where are the bairns ? " he demanded the minute they got indoors. As the little folks came, in response to their mother's call, they, with the quick intuition of childhood, hailed and welcomed a new friend. He knew their names in a trice, ay, their pet names too ; he knew their ages, and the things they liked and the things they did not like. Even Bobby, the Manse dog, an animal of supernatural sagacity and a variety of breeds, greeted him " like a long lost brother " as the Doctor said.

" Come away," he cried gaily, leading the way into the dining-room, " come and see what's in this baggie ! " They gathered round him with happy, excited faces, and of the little group the Doctor was certainly the blithest and the youngest. Not since the grim shadow of the minister's illness had fallen on the Manse had there been such gaiety. And the contents of that precious bag ? Chocolate animals, butterscotch, a toy bull dog of ferocious aspect (it was only Bobby's sense of politeness which prevented his biting this fearsome beast), sweets of large and satisfying dimensions ! What bliss !

The meal which followed partook more of the nature of a feast than of an ordinary diet, and that not because the fare was anything great or grand, but because the Doctor sat at the end of the table and kept everyone happy and laughing. How he discovered Bobby's weakness for sugar no one could tell, but the knowing little dog was discovered beneath the Doctor's chair crunching a lump of sugar with noisy enthusiasm, and laughing at the jokes too.

In the midst of the fun the postman's ring sounded

through the house, and the maid handed in a long flat parcel. Mrs. Urquhart took a hasty glance at it and saw that the writing was her husband's ; then, determined to " mind her manners," she laid it on the sideboard. The Doctor's bright eyes had quite taken in the little scene, and after a minute or two he said with a pawky smile, " Is that a parcel from himsell ? "

Mrs. Urquhart blushed guiltily. Perhaps " minding her manners " had not included keeping her eyes from wandering wistfully to the parcel ! " Would you like me to cut the string ? " he inquired, opening his penknife. " As a rule I'm against sinful waste, but under present circumstances (you've gazed longingly at that parcel ten times !) I think we're quite justified in being reckless." The wisdom of the man ! In a twinkling the string was cut, the paper off, and a blue card-board box came to view. Now, if you expect to hear that the minister's wife got a diamond pendant or a string of pearls, you had better read no more of this homely tale ; for what was lying there wrapped up in tissue paper was nothing more nor less than a white silk blouse and a pretty scarf !

And because that stupid woman had been feeling wretchedly anxious and worried about " himsell," and a little forlorn too, she felt her eyes fill with sudden blinding tears as she peered into the box. The Doctor did not see this, of course ! " Tut, tut, tut," he grumbled. " The idea ! the extravagant man ! " He was fingering the wonderful garment as gently as if it were a new-born baby. " The silly boy," he went on ; " why, he might have bought vegetarian cookery books for the cannibals, or picture hats for the Esquimaux— or—or—let me see now—why, bombs for the suffragettes, with his money—but what does he do ? Buys a blouse for his wife instead ! I'll report him to the Presbytery ! You won't, of course, be wearing it to-morrow ? " he asked anxiously.

" But indeed I shall ! " she flashed defiantly.

He sighed and shook his head. " I'll pray for you,"

he promised. "I'll pray that this hand-maiden *be not puffed up!* Well, well, is that a letter I see below the wonderful blouse? Just let me hear how he is—and then would you like me to have worship before the little folks go to bed?"

God seemed wonderfully near that evening as they gathered round the table, Bibles in hand. The Doctor got the children, one by one, to read a verse, and then he asked the maid—he knew her name already—to read one too. When the youngest boy read in his clear high voice that "the 'Scribes and Paraphrases' came to Jesus," it did not seem such a deadly mistake—because the smile on the Doctor's face was wholly tender. In the prayer which followed, he wrapped the little band in loving petitions—that their eyes might be kept from tears (one at least of his hearers knew why he thus prayed). "For earthly love which binds husband and wife, parent and child, brother and sister, we thank Thee," and then ended with his favourite petition, "Take us under the shadow of Thy wings, that there we may abide all the days of our life until the end." The hush and spell of the Unseen filled the room and made it a holy place as he poured out his heart to his Heavenly Father, just as fully and as freely as a child speaks to a loving earthly father.

.   .   .   .

Sabbath morning dawned clear and cloudless. The snow had evidently changed its mind and had gone elsewhere. The sea sparkled merrily in the sunshine, and a courageous lark was singing joyously in a field near the Manse. "This is the day which the Lord hath made," the old Doctor read, and then lifting his eyes from the Bible he gazed out at the sunny world. "And it's like Him," he said reverently, and as if thinking aloud, "It's like Him!"

Of the old Doctor in the pulpit I feel I cannot speak. He came before the congregation with the careful fruit of his week's study—the old truth new minted, and bearing upon it the stamp and sparkle of heaven. His text was, " Sir, we would see Jesus," and before his words the folks swayed like corn in an autumn breeze. A little boy, sitting in the Manse seat, suddenly slipped his hand into his mother's and whispered, " Is he seeing Jesus ? Surely he's seeing Jesus. I wish I could see Him too ! " Yes, if the pure in heart see God, the old Doctor was certainly seeing Jesus, and many a soul that Sabbath morning felt the sin and sorrow, the tiredness and the weariness of the past, smitten away, as they too drew near to catch, if they might, a glimpse of Jesus. Recapturing the joy of their first coming, they said once more, " Sir, we would see Jesus." It was a great day.

In the evening the church was packed. The crowd inspired the Doctor, and never, even in his younger days, had he preached with more passion and fervour. " And He showed me a pure river of life clear as crystal," and " Let him that is athirst come . . . and drink." He bracketed the gracious words, and from them wove such a wonderful appeal that hard indeed must the heart have been which did not respond. As the folks sang the closing psalm they showed they had been moved and touched. They sang with their hearts, and that is the best of all singing ;

> " A river is, whose streams do glad
>   The City of our God ;
> The holy place, wherein the Lord
>   Most High hath His abode."

The old Doctor stood in the pulpit singing too, the light from the pulpit lamps shining down on his reverend white head and saintly face, and, as he lifted his hands in blessing, it seemed to the breathless crowd that his face was as the face of an angel.

> " Oh, may we stand before the Lamb
>   When earth and seas are fled,
> And hear the Judge pronounce our name
>   With blessings on our head,"

he pleaded, and a great inarticulate " Amen " welled up in every listening heart.

As the Doctor walked to the Manse after the service he suddenly became conscious of overpowering weariness. " There is no preaching without the shedding of blood," he thought as he slowly went home. A young man who had been in church that evening was coming behind him, and because his heart had been thrilled and touched by the service, and because the Doctor always brought out the best in everyone—that young man, who was naturally a shy and diffident youth, said, as he came alongside the minister, " Sir, will you allow me to offer you my arm ? I am going your way."

The Doctor's tired face blossomed into instant and joyous youth.

" My dear boy, how good of you ! Certainly I'll be glad of your arm. Do you know," he lowered his voice and spoke confidentially, " I'm like the devil, I'm old ; but I'm not infirm, only a little tired." Certainly no one hearing his merry laugh would think he was either old or infirm.

" I'm like the devil in another way," he went on, evidently finding much pleasure in these comparisons. " I must be in earnest for my time is brief. Ah, my boy, what an opportunity I had to-night to speak to all that crowd of young folks, and how I prayed the Father that He would give me the right word to say to you all ! "

They walked on in silence, and just because the young man's heart was so full, his obstinate tongue refused to help him with so much as a single word. Perhaps the Doctor understood, for presently he began speaking about the wonders of the stars. A new moon, a lovely crescent, hung in the sky, and a golden star swung over its cup. Astronomy had always fascinated him, and he delighted the listening lad with his marvellous knowledge of this science, for the old Doctor was always a scholar.

" Well, my boy, here we are at the Manse gate, and I've enjoyed the walk. You must tell me your name, and I'll send you a little book on astronomy, seeing you are interested in it too. Write me any time you think I can help you in any way. It will give me great pleasure." And it was no idle promise, as the future proved.

The Manse children had begged as a special favour to be allowed to sit up and have supper with Dr. Lindsay, and now as his step sounded on the garden path they flew to open the door, headed by Bobby. One helped him off with his coat, another relieved him of his umbrella, his gloves were pulled off—I grieve to say that afterwards Bobby was seen to suffocate himself with one, under the impression it was a rabbit! The Doctor's slippers were toasting inside the fender, and his energetic little friends unlaced his boots and thrust his feet into the warm slippers before he had had time to fetch his breath. When he did he quoted with twinkling eyes :

> " And now if e'er by chance I put
>   My finger into glue,
>   Or madly crush my right-hand foot
>   Into my left-hand shoe
>   I weep . . ."

But he got no further, for with a shout of delight the children saw that they had indeed crushed his " right-hand foot into his left-hand shoe," and they proceeded to put matters right.

Supper past, they gathered round the table, and I wish I could show you the Doctor and those happy young folks around him, and how each in turn read a verse ; and then how the Doctor asked, could someone play a hymn, and how someone could, and did, and how the voices old and young joined in the sweetest of all the psalms :

> " The Lord's my shepherd, I'll not want."

Then with a short word of prayer, commending all

loved ones to the Shepherd who " neither slumbers nor sleeps," the Doctor finished.

. . . .

After the children had gone to bed, he and Mrs. Urquhart sat by the study fire and talked. It is only those who have had the privilege of spending a Sabbath evening with him who know what a delightful thing that was. He was a man of widest sympathy and most generous disposition. He was far too big souled to descend to petty jealousy, and his warm appreciation of his fellow-ministers, and loyalty to his Church, were among his most lovable traits. His spirit loved to dwell on heaven and on the life there. Dr. Barnardo's life had just been published, and speaking of it he said : " I have no time to read it, much as I should like to ; but no matter—when I get to heaven I'll hear all about it from Dr. Barnardo himself."

" May I put my feet up on the side of the mantelpiece ? I can tell from those marks that ' himsell ' is allowed to do so. Thank you. It gives the dog more room, you see, and it rests my back, and also gives me a chance to show off my grand new socks." And then he told her the story of the socks.

Some time before he had been visiting in the country. The night was dark and the way long, and he suddenly bethought him that by crossing a burn he might shorten his road. Alas, the burn was in spate, and the plank which usually served as a bridge had been washed to the further side. This did not " daunten " the Doctor in the least, and with an " Ouch " at the coldness of the water he waded to the other side. His way now took him past the farm of Burnside, but ere coming to the farm-house he had to pass the ploughmen's bothies. He heard, as he approached the nearest one, the notes of " a cheery wee melodeon " played with much taste and a fine disregard for time. In a lull in the music he tapped at the door, and was bidden " Come in." When he opened the door he saw gathered round a cosy wood fire three or four young fellows listening to the musician

who sat in state on the table. The lads looked a little
" blate " when they saw a minister, but before his genial
smile the awkwardness soon fled.

" Will you let an old man dry his feet at your fire,
boys ? " he asked.

Would they ? The boys rose as one man, and in a
trice the Doctor was seated in front of the roasting fire ;
the musician leapt off his perch and began rummaging
in the " shottle " of his kist for something which he
presently offered—not without blushing ; the herd loon,
who had been whittling a whistle out of a " sappy sucker
frae the muckle rodden tree," knelt down and undid the
wet boots and set them on the hobs to dry. The
cattleman, who was a married man and initiated in
domestic mysteries, took the wet socks and wrung them
out at the door. It was then the musician screwed up
courage to offer his treasure. It was a pair of socks of
chaste and quiet colours (green and red), and round
their tops had been woven by some magic art the
touching words " Remember me." The Doctor donned
them with great alacrity, for there was no one who could
more graciously accept a kindness—a much more
difficult business than bestowing one !

Then they talked, and you can guess who was the
merriest there. The musician, with outward humility
and inward pride, played the Doctor's favourite tune,
which was—but no ! that was to be a secret ! Then
the talk came round to work days and rest days, and
the day of rest, and how did they spend it. The little
company were serious now, for the native dignity of the
Doctor always kept everyone in his own place. " I'll
read a chapter with you, boys," he said, " and then I
must be going." Again it was the musician who dived
into his kist and brought out a Bible wrapped in a piece
of tissue paper. The Doctor examined it carefully. " I
would like to see it looking as if it were oftener used, my
boy. I see it was your mother who gave it to you. Did
she tell you to keep it wrapped up in your trunk ? Is
she still alive ? "

"No, sir. Yes, sir." Robbie Kemp, horseman and musician in ordinary to the farm of Burnside, answered.

In the prayer which followed, the Doctor prayed that he and they, their fathers and their mothers, might meet in the Homeland to which we are daily drawing nearer, and the listening lads resolved that come what might they would go to church next Sunday and write home to the old folks too.

By this time the boots and socks were dry, and while the Doctor was getting into them, Willie, the herd loon, vanished suddenly. He came back in a minute with his stable lantern in his hand, and was nearly felled by the musician for his pains. "I'm to take my bicycle lamp," he whispered fiercely. "Be off and supper your bastes."

I do not know how many of the lads convoyed him home, nor how many lamps they carried—the Doctor would never tell. "But there!" he added triumphantly, "these are the socks that Robbie Kemp's sweetheart made for me, and I'm prouder of them than a gardener's dog with a rose in its tail! I'm to marry them, too, whenever Robbie can get a married man's place, and I think I know a farmer that's needing just such a man as Robbie."

That was the story of the socks, and it was not difficult to read between the lines, nor to guess that because of "him who passed by" that evening and turned aside for a little into the bothy of Burnside, the whole course of Robbie Kemp's after-life was altered.

"But I must be going to bed," he said, glancing at the clock. "Can you give me the change for half a crown before I go?"

"No," she said promptly, "I can't"; and then, greatly daring, she said, "You know you don't need change for half a crown. You have your return ticket."

The Doctor threw his eyes and hands ceiling-wards. "Did ever any mortal hear such impudence?" he inquired of some unseen hearer. "I don't need change, quo' she! Well, well."

"No, you don't," she repeated. "You are just wanting to give money to some one, and you're not to."

His eyes twinkled mischievously. "But I will get change—if I have to knock up the treasurer of the church to give it to me—I defy you, magerful woman, I won't be bullied by you." He thumped the table with his fist, and looked so exactly like a naughty child rejoicing in its naughtiness that of course it ended in laughter and the Doctor getting his own way. "I just wanted to leave a trifle for the maid," he explained.

When she came back with the change he was gazing dreamily into the heart of the glowing fire. "Do you know," he began, "I had such a strange dream last night—I think I must tell it to you. I dreamt I was in heaven, and the queer thing was that I didn't feel a bit happier than I had done many a time on earth. There was not a kent face to be seen, and I felt lonely—dreadfully lonely. But just then I noticed a young man by my side, a tall dignified looking man with a friendly open face.

"'You have just come?' he said.

"'Yes, sir,' I answered.

"'And are you feeling a little lonely?'

"'Well—yes—I was a little lonely; but since you have spoken to me, that feeling has gone.'

"'Would you like Me to stay with you?' he asked. His eyes were wonderful, as if at some time in His life He had known some great tragedy, and on His brow was the mark of an old wound.

"'Sir,' I said, 'it is what I would like above everything else, *I feel—I feel as if I had known You all my life.*'

"He stretched out His hand to greet me. There was the mark of an old wound in its palm; when I looked into His face He was smiling; and then—then—I knew it—was—the—Lord Himself!"

.   .   .   .

The old Doctor has passed many years ago. He has entered that Heaven home to which his thoughts went forth while he dwelt among us, and who can doubt that the first to meet and greet him in the new home would be no other than his life-long friend in the old—the tall young man with the scarred brow and nail-pierced hands—the Lord Himself !

THE WEDDING PARTY AND THE DOCTOR

THE "happy couple" had departed, and we, the wedding guests, were left to entertain each other till such time as our various trains and 'buses were due. Most of us were strangers to each other, and the somewhat formal and unhomely air of the hotel drawing-room where we had met certainly did not tend to make us more genial.

I had slipped into a window-seat and was furtively studying a motorists' guide to Perthshire. In imagination I was just negotiating a difficult bend on the Crieff road, when a voice close beside me startled me by saying, "Aren't you the lady who wrote about the Doctor?"

A tall handsome lady whom I had been admiring from a distance, but whose name I did not know, was preparing to share my window-seat. She had the most charming smile, with just a hint of mischief in it which reminded one of the remark made by Robert Louis Stevenson's father to Fanny, his wife, "I doot ye're a beesom!" Her next speech proved that this surmise was correct, for she said, with a little ripple of laughter, "He married me!"

She seemed rather disappointed that I was not more shocked, and presently she went on, "Yes, he married me, and baptised our children, and—and——" She paused, and I knew from her face that her mind was thronging with old, fond, glad memories. "I often wonder at the folks God entrusts children to," she said, with, as it were, a farewell wave to some old, happy recollection. "When I think what an ignorant young mother I was, I wonder my poor little baby didn't die. He used to roar himself red in the face, trying to tell me how much he disapproved of my methods! I remember one evening he was particularly noisy. He was making

such a row that I never heard the door opening, nor
knew that the Doctor was standing close beside me.   He
picked up the young rascal, perched him on his shoulder,
and began marching up and down the nursery floor
with him.   The child was so amazed, he broke off in
the middle of a lusty roar, in pure astonishment, and was
so pleased with his new nurse, he never began again.
The Doctor said, ' You're not the first young mother
whom I have taught to hold a baby.   You plant the
child right up on your shoulder—but go for your husband.   I may as well teach you both when I'm at it.'   I
wondered afterwards if the Doctor knew that I was tired,
and whether he took this plan just to get my husband to
do his share of nursing.   It would be like him !   He
often used to look in, after that, and I never knew anyone who had such a way with babies.   That's the baby
the Doctor taught me how to hold," she said, nodding
laughingly towards a tall young fellow who was standing
near the door.

He looked, one grieves to say, as if he were about to
do a flanking movement to the rear ; but, catching his
mother's eye, he joined her in the window.   I could tell
from the way he carried himself that he had been a
soldier.

" I have been telling what a noisy little chap you
used to be, Donald," she said, after introducing us,
" and how the Doctor showed me the proper way to
hold you."

Mother and son exchanged understanding looks.
Then I knew why she was still " a beesom " ; it was
because her boy and herself were chums.

" I can hardly believe you were ever small enough for
anyone to carry you," I said, looking at this young
giant.

" Oh, but he was," his mother said briskly, " and used
to wear frocks and bibs."

" Now, mother ! " the lad protested, " that wasn't
my fault.   I can remember quite well how the Doctor
comforted me by telling me I'd be a man before my

mother. It was he who congratulated me on my first pair of knickers (or were they shorts ?).''

" They looked short enough," his mother jeered, " especially from behind ! "

Her son affected not to hear, and went on :

" I was only allowed one pocket in those days, and the Doctor put a penny in it."

" Was it a hip pocket ? " I asked curiously.

" How did you guess ? " he laughed. " It was."

" It was about the size of a penny postage stamp," his mother reminded him sweetly. And then we all rocked with laughter.

It was strange how warm and friendly the air of the room had grown. We made a place for Donald to sit down beside us. He seemed to have forgotten he had planned a retreat, and we prepared for " a good old chin wag." The phrase was his, also the complaint that, as his feet were of the " two-feet-one-back-yard " measurement, it was impossible for him to tuck them out of sight.

I liked this Donald from the beginning ; he was such an understanding sort of a boy. And when he spoke, it was to tell of his great school-chum, one Sandy Macleod, who also had been great friends with the Doctor. Both the boys had been in the habit of doing their lessons together ; their homes were side by side. They began Latin the same term, and were not at all sure they liked it. One evening Sandy was grinding up the declensions, when he heard, as he imagined, Donald opening the outer door.

" Come in quietly," he shouted, " wipe your feet, and be quick about it. I'm at my Latin ! "

Slowly the door squeaked open, there was the sound of someone wiping his feet with elaborate care, and then—in marched the Doctor !

" I think my boots are quite clean ! " he said cheerfully. " I wiped them twelve times. Look ! "

Poor Sandy, with a crimson face, was stammering out

apologies which the Doctor brushed aside with, " Let's have a look at the Latin grammar."

A post-card with the Macleod motto, " *Murus aheneus esto,*" was lying on the table, and the Doctor read it aloud, with a merry twinkle in his eyes.

" It means," he said, " that the Macleods are a brazen-faced people. Now, the next time I come here, if you attend to your Latin, you'll be able to tell me if my translation is correct."

Sandy always declared that it was the Doctor who gave him his love for Latin, and to this day Sandy's versions are spoken of with respect in his old school. Also, he was able to tell his old friend that the Macleod motto meant, " Be thou a brazen wall ! "

" Where is Sandy now ? " I asked.

Donald looked out of the window for what seemed a long time, and then he said : " In . . . France. You remember . . . Messines . . . June . . . 1917 ?   It was then."

*   *   *   *   *   *

Presently he went on :

" You remember the first time *The Doctor* was published ? My folks sent me a copy in the Christmas parcel, and I lent it to Sandy who lent it to another Morayshire ' loon.'   Indeed, *The Doctor* went up and down the line all that week, till at last it fell into the hands of Jock Tulloch. Jock was a wild character, but a first-rate soldier. His language, when the Germans began their evening ' strafe,' was so picturesque it received honourable mention from all the rank and file of the British Army ! Yet this particular evening it was noticed he never said a word.

" ' Fit's this you're reading ? ' his nearest neighbour asked, trying to squint over Jock's shoulder.

" Jock glowered dazedly at him like a man wakening out of a deep sleep. Then, after a bit, he cried, ' Oh. man, man, I thocht this hell o' a place was a' a bad dream, an' that I was back again in Elgin, going aff to

play fit-ba' in the Cooper Park.' He began to fasten
his coat more tightly, and to touch aimlessly his rifle.
His voice was a hoarse whisper when he went on :
' It was me that began ma fit-ba' days wi' a syrup tin ;
it was me that made the Doctor break a' the eggs.'
You see, Jock was ' that limb o' Tulloch's ' who played
a match with the old Doctor one famous March morning.
All that night Jock's mind was full of home, and he
spoke again and again of Elgin. In the morning . . .
he went home ; the twin brothers Death and Sleep
carried him there, though a German bullet hit him in the
head. . . . This is queer news for a wedding party,"
Donald said briskly.

An elderly man who looked like a farmer had joined
us by this time.

"You're speaking about the Doctor," he said,
admitting quite frankly that he had been listening.
' Ay, ay, I like to hear his verra name ! He used to
come an' see me when I was in bed wi' a broken leg, an'
whiles he found me ill-natured, an' whiles he found me
real doon-herted, but he aye left me cheery ! One day
he cam' wearin' a braw new tweed suit ; for the most
pairt he wore a stan' o' blacks, an' when he was goin'
awa', says he, ' Ye've never said a wird aboot ma new
claes, James.' ' An',' says I, ' I think they're real
becomin'. Noo that ye mention them yirsell, I must
tell ye sae ; afore I did na like tae.' He took a haud o'
the tails o' the jacket, an' spreadin' them oot says he,
' *Neat-but-not-gaudy*, as the deil said about his new tail.' "

By this time the window was getting too small to hold
us, and when tea was fetched in we gathered sociably
round the fire. The table-maid who attended to our
wants seemed to spend an unnecessarily long time over
her duties, and I could not help wondering whether she
was listening to the talk ; for everyone now had some
cherished story to relate.

There was one especially touching one, told by a
quiet-looking lady who was a nurse. She had had a
case of nervous break-down to tend, and perhaps there

is no more trying malady to nurse. Her patient simply
could not sleep, and doctor and nurse were at their wits'
end. One evening, in desperation, she took up a little
book and read aloud the first chapter. To her delight
the patient, who had been tossing restlessly, lay quite
still, listening eagerly. " Oh, nurse, do go on," she
begged, when the first chapter was finished. " If you
will try to go to sleep now, I'll read you the next one
when you waken," the nurse promised. The curious
thing was that this was the turning point in the illness ;
the patient slept all that evening, the first natural sleep
she had had for weeks.

How I wished I could have told our old friend this
story, and yet is it not possible that he knows better far
than anyone can tell ?

Our little company had begun to " skail " now, as
one after another took their departure. We were
loth to part, and I was especially sorry when Donald
and his mother went. Ships that pass in the night,
perhaps, but how kindly the greeting, how warm the
memory ! The old farmer and myself were the last
to go.

I must tell again one of his stories. It was one the
Doctor was fond of relating, and I can well imagine the
wicked delight with which he would tell it in certain
company. An old minister had, for an assistant, an
exceedingly stiff and starchy young man. He sent him
one day to officiate at a funeral. The poor man, feeling
like a fish out of water, was trying to utter what he
considered suitable remarks. To a man sitting near
him, he said :

" What—was—the—occupation—of—our—departed
—brother ? "

" I—I beg your pardon," the man said, in much
alarm.

" What—ah—was the calling or—ah—occupation—
of our departed—friend ? "

The man pondered the remark for a little, then his
face suddenly cleared.

" I see what you're at, sir. I say, Jock," addressing a man on the other side of the room, "*fit wis the corp to trade ?* "

*   *   *   *   *   *

With many hand-shakings and many promises of meeting again, the old farmer and myself parted, the last of the wedding guests. In the cloakroom, the table-maid came stealing in.

" Excuse me," she whispered, " I couldn't help hearing you speaking about the Doctor. I—I loved him too. When my brother was dying, he used to come every Saturday night and tell him what he was going to preach about next day. Then, when my sister Phemie and myself were left alone—oh, he was good to us ! Phemie went to Australia to get married. She got a good man, but she never kept well. The Doctor died after Phemie went away, and I felt as if I could not tell her the sad news. I planned to go to Australia myself, for Phemie was homesick and I was lonely too. Then I sent her your little book, and when she had to lie in bed, she used to take it with her to read. The neighbours were kind to her, and we were hoping, once I got out and nursed her, that she would get strong again. One day her sister-in-law came to tidy up, and she took a good while putting things right. ' Are you thinking long, Phemie ? ' she asked, when she was through. But Phemie didn't answer. She did not move either. She was lying as if she were asleep, with a smile on her face, and gripped tight in her hand was the wee book. It was open at the place where he tells the bonnie dream he had, and of how he felt at home when ' the tall young man with the scarred brow and the nail-pierced hands—the Lord Himself,' was there. . . . Phemie must have been feeling that she was going home too . . . for she was smiling. . . . They buried her with the wee book in her hand. . . . I'm—glad."

"So am I," I said, fumbling for my handkerchief.

All the way home I had the company of the Doctor. "Dead," they say? "Nay, I cannot think of him as that. Rather does he rest from his labours, but—HIS WORKS DO FOLLOW HIM."

Printed by The Whitefriars Press, Ltd., London and Tonbridge.